Darkness over Cannae by J.N. Dolfen
Cover by J. N. Dolfen
This edition published in 20202

Zmok Books is an imprint of

Winged Hussar Publishing, LLC
1525 Hulse Rd, Unit 1
Point Pleasant, NJ 08742

Copyright © Zmok Books
ISBN 978-1-950423-09-5
LCN 2020951954

Bibliographical References and Index
1. Historical Fiction. 2. Ancient Rome. 3. Military

Winged Hussar Publishing, LLC All rights reserved
For more information
visit us at www.wingedhussarpublishing.com

Twitter: WingHusPubLLC
Facebook: Winged Hussar Publishing LLC

DARKNESS OVER CANNAE

J.N. Dolfen

ZMOK
BOOKS

The year is 216 BC.
As Rome and Carthage vie for supremacy,
the Mediterranean is shaken by a conflict
that will go down in history
as the Second Punic War.

Two years ago,
Hannibal, the Carthaginian general,
took Rome completely by surprise
by leading an army
of African, Spanish, and Celtic soldiers
across the Alps
to attack Rome on her own soil.

Rome has suffered three defeats
at his hands already,
and spent the last year licking her wounds
and avoiding another battle.

Now, the senate in Rome feels the time has come to
take the initiative again.

With an army of an unprecedented eight legions,
led by both consuls and two proconsuls,
they are determined to put Hannibal in his place
once and for all.

"Wake me an hour before dawn," Bomilkar son of Balal muttered to himself in exasperation. "Wish he'd said where, exactly."

The torch in his hand was just barely bright enough to find his way through the outskirts of the sleeping Punic camp, and avoid walking into propped-up shields, sleepers, and the occasional pile of horse droppings. It was an early morning in high summer, the third year of the campaign, and the Roman army, over eighty thousand strong if the disconcerting rumours were to be believed, was encamped ten stades from the Punic.

Battle was in the air, had been for days; and Bomilkar, chief of Hannibal's bodyguard, was searching for the general.

Hannibal was not in his tent, and the guard outside had told Bomilkar that he hadn't slept there at all, but had left for the outer guard posts an hour after midnight. This was hardly new behaviour, but Bomilkar wished the general didn't do this on a day when battle was likely. Sometimes, he wondered whether Hannibal was doing this on purpose, just to keep him on his feet. As if he ever wasn't. He could pride himself on having seen Hannibal mostly unscathed through alpine ambushes and two battles, as well as several skirmishes against Roman armies.

The sky was still the deep indigo of the summer night; in the east, a strip of paler blue was creeping up on the horizon, heralding the dawn. Barely a cloud in the sky – the day would be hot, just like that last, and the one before that.

Guards were sitting or standing at watchfires, talking quietly, turning as he passed. Some conversations Bomilkar understood; many were in languages he didn't know, in some cases, couldn't even place. There were Numidians, Gaetulans, Moors, Libyans, Libyphoenicians and Qart-hadasht townspeople from North Africa; Iberians, Celtiberians, Baleareans and Lusitans from Iberia and the islands; Ligurians and Gauls from the north of Italy and southern Gaul, and a bunch of small contingents from Illyria, south Italy, even Macedon and Greece and a dozen places Bomilkar had never heard of, that had joined Hannibal's enterprise over the last two years.

He hadn't gone far before a few Gaetulans waved him over and directed him to a watchfire further on, telling him, in broken Punic, that Hannibal was there. They were grinning. Yes, Bomilkar decided, he was doing this on purpose.

He found the general asleep at the fire, covered with his cloak, his back propped against a rock. The guards at this fire were Balearic slingers, for which Bomilkar was grateful. Those people had absolutely no sense of humour, and so they didn't break out in mirth at the sight of the chief guard tracking down his charge. The men were dressed in short tunics, with spare slings tied around heads and waists as girdles and headbands. They were cooking porridge for breakfast, and Bomilkar was reminded that he hadn't eaten yet.

He bent down to lightly shake Hannibal's shoulder. "You said to wake you. The sun will come up soon."

Hannibal started slightly, twisting around. "I told you not to creep up on my right." He rubbed his dead right eye.

Bomilkar shook his head. "Have you been out here all night?" he asked disapprovingly.

"No, not quite," Hannibal replied. He got to his feet in a seamless motion and turned to the small pinpoints of firelight burning further north along the river Aufidus. "Anything stirring over there yet?"

Bomilkar followed the general's gaze. The Roman army was so large that it was accommodated in two camps – the larger one on this side of the river, and another on the opposite bank. "They've sounded the trumpets, but other than that, all quiet," the guard replied. He eyed Hannibal. "Will we fight today?"

"Yes," Hannibal said simply, stretching. "They didn't want to come out yesterday, but there's no way they'll keep this up today. Varro won't risk his soldiers thinking him a coward, even less than Paullus."

He appeared as calm as Bomilkar had ever seen him before a battle, never betraying the slightest amount of apprehension, at least none that Bomilkar had ever been able to discern. The general turned to look at the sky, and Bomilkar saw him pause at a spot in the north-west, where the sky was still completely dark.

"Do you see that?" Hannibal asked as he became aware of his guard captain's quizzical look.

"What is it?"

Hannibal gave a chuckle. "I'd have expected you, of all people, to know the constellation of Melqart, as he is your name patron." He pointed it out to Bomilkar. "My father used to show him to me, many years ago. I have rarely seen him as clearly in the sky as tonight."

"Won't the Romans see him as a good omen too?"

"Maybe they'd like to." Hannibal smiled. It was no secret that he had adopted Melqart, called Hercules by the Romans, as his guiding patron for the war against Rome, and many compared the general openly to the hero, who, too, had crossed the Alps on his way to Italy. "But I think he's made it clear which side he favours, don't you think?"

He nodded his thanks to one of the men, who handed him a wooden bowl with porridge. Bomilkar smelled olive oil and salt fish, and his stomach gave a distinct rumble.

The general turned to the Baleareans. "Give the poor man something to eat," he said in Iberian, with a wink at Bomilkar. "It's just like him to have everything covered, except his stomach. Ikorbas, go to the outpost at the northern gate and have the trumpets sounded. Tell them to send out twelve fast riders, to watch out for any activity in the Roman camp. Whatever happens, I want to know immediately." The slinger acknowledged the order, and hurried off.

Bomilkar gratefully accepted a second bowl, and they ate. Rations were short, but Hannibal always made sure that everyone ate properly the morning before battle. The difficulty, recently, had been to determine when exactly "the morning before battle" was.

Hannibal had deployed his army on the left bank the day before, but Paullus, one of the two Roman consuls commanding, had declined to come out and meet the challenge. Today, it would be his colleague's day of command. De-spite their marked lack of enthusiasm on the previous day, everyone knew that the consuls had come here to fight. The days of Fabius the Delayer were over.

"Why do you think they didn't fight yesterday?" Bomilkar asked, his mouth full. He had spoken Punic; like most Libyan soldiers who had spent a decade or so in Iberia, he understood Iberian, and most of the men in Hannibal's army had a working knowledge of Punic, but conversations around the tents tended to be a curious mishmash of a dozen different languages; three dozen if you counted the mutually intelligible dialects. Compiling lists of more than fifty faecal words and insults was a favourite pastime that never got old.

"Why? Perhaps they couldn't pull the standards from the ground again. Or maybe the sacred chickens wouldn't eat. If we keep beating them, they'll be running out of lucky portents soon." Hannibal had reverted to Iberian for the

Baleareans' benefit; two of them laughed, to Bomilkar's amazement.

"Ah, Paullus doesn't trust me," Hannibal went on to Bomilkar, again in Punic. "He must have been worried I had an ambush site prepared. Though where he thinks I'd find one in a wide open plain is anyone's guess. He probably thinks I carry them around in the baggage train."

"That would come in handy here," said Bomilkar, his voice tight.

"What, because of those eight legions?" Hannibal said. "Don't worry. Three hundred Spartans were enough for a hundred thousand Persians at the battle of Thermopylai."

"They had a narrow gorge."

"Well, yes. But we have something better."

Bomilkar looked over the plains to his right, which were now slowly becoming visible, half-expecting ravines or woods to appear there by magic. Truth be told, there was little he would put past Hannibal's miracle-working capacities. He had led them across the Alps, he had beaten the Romans repeatedly on their own soil, and he had made Baleareans laugh. "What's that?" he asked.

Hannibal clapped him on the back and grinned. "Me."

He turned to the men around the campfire, handing his empty bowl back to one of them. "I'm off to make the rounds. Bomilkar, gather your men together and come to my command tent. I want the commanding officers there before sunrise. The inner circle plus Qarthalo, Monomachos, Gisgo, and the council elders." He clapped his hands. "Let's get to it."

"So the decision stands."

"Of course the decision stands. Haven't you heard the augurs, Paullus? And you a pontifex yourself – what more could you hope for?"

Lucius Aemilius Paullus didn't answer his colleague at once, his jaws working. "I'm not arguing against the good omens. Just give us a few more days, at least. If we wait until the enemy is forced to move away for lack of food, we could even intercept him on the march."

Gaius Terentius Varro shook his head emphatically. "Intercept Hannibal on the march? With his small, fast army?"

"At the very least, it enables us to learn more about him."

"What do you want to know?" Varro said sharply. "We know everything about him. He has played us for fools for two years, he has won two victories through ambushes and treachery, we've got him cornered, and we outnumber him five to three. What more could you possibly expect to learn? Or is it that you wish to wait one more day, or three, or five, so glory can be yours?"

Paullus stood silently, and Varro gave him a grim look that said, *Of course you do.*

The two consuls were alone in Varro's command tent, or Paullus would not have spoken so plainly. Varro had just supervised the sacrifices; augurs and haruspices were agreed that the omens were excellent. Still, the idea of fighting today filled Aemilius Paullus with unease. It was not only that he would have loved to be in command on the day when Hannibal was finally fought and beaten. He told himself it was foolish, after months of preparing the great strike that would smash the Carthaginian's army and bring an end to this war, but now that the day was here, he felt rushed.

"Even if we decided to delay," Varro went on, "How would you explain that to the men? We have eighty-six thousand men out there who would rather bite off a finger than wait for a single day longer. And we'll run out of food much sooner than Hannibal will, with his smaller army and with the granary he's captured. He forages at will and his cavalry won't let our foragers do the same. His very presence here in this field is an outrage. No, Paullus, no. This has to end. Today, we fight. Today, we win."

Paullus groped for arguments that might sway Varro, but he knew his arguments were shaky at best.

His colleague watched him for a moment, before calling to the guard outside his tent as he stepped through the entrance. "Fly the red *vexillum*," he  called out aloud, to cheers from the men near them, "and blow the trumpets. The omens have never been better. Today, Rome will march forth!"

"Terentius." Paullus hastened after him and held his colleague by the arm, speaking in a low voice. "I know that the left bank is out of the question – but I'm not happy about the right. It favours the enemy's cavalry too much."

"You don't want to fight on level ground for your fear of his cavalry. You don't want to fight on rough terrain for your fear of ambushes." Varro had come to a halt in the semi-privacy of the tent entrance. "Where, in your opinion, should we give battle? On the bottom of the sea? Or on treetops?"

"In a place where we know *he* can't stage an ambush, and that we have controlled for about a week before he gets there!" Paullus answered between his teeth. "He has been here for weeks! What do you think he has been doing?"

"Such a situation will never happen!" Varro ground out. "We cannot force him to fight. You know that as well as I do. He's a lot more mobile than we are."

"But he can force *us* to fight?"

Varro snorted in exasperation. "The gods know why he even wants to fight here, outnumbered as he is! We need to take this chance, and beat him now, before he realises he has overreached himself! Aemilius, why won't you see it – Hannibal has finally made a mistake. He is not forcing us to fight; we've brought the fox to bay! Today, *I* am choosing the battle ground. We finally have him where we want him, and we can finally end this. And by Jupiter Stator, I will. It's the great deeds and courage of our ancestors that have made Rome great, and that will save her now. Not hiding, not hesitating, and certainly not bickering!"

Varro fell silent. Paullus found himself breathing hard.

"We have been over this," Varro said, in an assuaging tone. "We will not get a better chance than here, and now. Not only the omens, all the odds are better than anything has ever been in this war. We've just been too blind to see it. We will not repeat the mistakes of the past, you and I."

Paullus made no reply. Yes, Varro's omens, Varro's choice of the battle ground. Three years ago, Terentius Varro had just been a praetor under Paullus' command, during the war in Illyria. Now, his then-subordinate would turn the tides and be remembered as the victor over Hannibal. The thought rankled, though Paullus had to concede that Varro was no longer his subordinate.

Varro seemed to have followed his colleague's line of thought. "Aemilius – while command is mine today, nobody will say we did not act in unison. I will defer to you the command of the citizen cavalry, as the elder."

Paullus pondered this. As the day of battle was set, command of the prestigious right wing was probably the greatest concession he could expect. Or maybe hope that Hannibal would sit in his camp and refuse to come out. But for some reason, he very much doubted this scenario.

At length, he nodded. "Agreed."

Varro slapped the pommel of the sword at his side, his face determined. "I'll lead out my men," he said. "As agreed, in close formation. Go back to your camp and then join me on the other side."

Paullus turned, summoning his bodyguard, who had waited outside the tent. Cornelius Lentulus was with them, a military tribune who also acted in the office of augur. "The auguries left nothing to be desired," the young man greeted the consul. He was still in the toga he had worn while taking the auspices. "Nothing will be left to chance today."

Paullus nodded. "Let us hope, my dear Lentulus. And what a good thing that the chickens were so hungry."

Lentulus met the consul's gaze uneasily.

"Oh, I would not suspect you to have ordered not to feed them since yesterday morning," Paullus went on. "Of course not. That would be sacrilege."

"Of course," Lentulus repeated. "Yes, the gods have made it clear that they're looking favourably on us today."

Paullus didn't press the matter. He wondered if Lentulus had acted on Varro's orders, or on his own initiative. He liked neither idea.

Both of them turned at the sound of trumpets as the *cornicines* in Varro's staff blew the signal for impending battle. There was no time to be wasted; even though he knew that it would take hours until the battle line was in position, there was so much to do, but one thing especially which the consul thought was most pressing.

"Lentulus," Paullus said, turning to the tribune. "Ride back to our camp at once, and lead out three *turmae* of cavalry. The second, fifth, and ninth of the Fifth Legion, I think. Scout the entire area right of the Aufidus. Be thorough, especially in places where an ambush might be hidden."

Lentulus' face made it plain that he thought this an unnecessary exercise. "The area is so flat that we could almost scout it entirely from here," he said. "The men will not..."

"The men will do as I command!" Paullus said sharply. "Within the last eighteen months, Sempronius lost a battle for lack of scouting. Flaminius lost his life, and an army. If there is one sentence I do not want to hear tonight, it is one that starts with 'If only'."

Lentulus seemed to swallow an objection, but mounted his horse and galloped off, his toga billowing behind him.

Paullus and his bodyguard also rode back across the river to the smaller camp. The sun was just rising; the sky was without a single cloud. Another good omen, Paullus thought, before he had to concede that the same sky hung over the Punic camp.

They rode along the *via principalis* to Paullus' purple command tent. The news that they would fight had travelled faster than the consul; everywhere, men were getting up and greeting Paullus, eager for battle.

"Good auguries, they say, Aemilius." Furius Bibaculus, his quaestor, awaited the consul in front of the tent, rubbing his hands, his eyes shining.

"True, Furius. Have the tribunes been called together? And Servilius?"

"Servilius should be on his way, as should be the tribunes."

"Good. We have some time; we have the shorter way to the battlefield. Tell the tribunes to wait here for me. Servilius is to assemble the Twelfth, to attack the Punic camp once battle has commenced, and find someone suitable to command it. Even if part of the enemy's army gets away, they'll be stranded without baggage and a rallying point." Furius acknowledged the order. Paullus dismounted, dismissed his bodyguards, and went into his tent.

He sent out the two servants, and passed over to the small *lararium*. He knelt in front of the humble earthen altar, lighting a few candles, then reached over his shoulder to draw up his cloak and cover his head.

"Lares, gods of my fathers," he said, quietly but clearly. "Cast away from us doubt and mistrust amongst ourselves. To you I commend myself and my army in this battle. Let me be a leader and an example to my men. Let me not be deceived by the treachery of the enemy." He hesitated, then continued, "And if I should meet my end this day, let me face it with courage and take my place among the honoured forefathers of the Aemilii." How hard it was to ask for blessing in this, of all matters. All the same, he avoided using the words *death* or *die* – to use them was to challenge bad luck, for himself and for those around him. Truth be told, he did not fear defeat this day. But to ignore the eventualities might anger the lares. Better by far to placate them, but not invoke the worst.

He took a pinch of salt from an earthen bowl, and sprinkled it over the candles. He stood and watched the crackling flame, then turned, shaking his cloak off his head, and went to assemble his troops.

Maharbal entered the command tent. Hannibal was not there yet; no doubt he was still making the rounds around the camp, to show off some confidence. He could do that in here again, too, Maharbal thought as he looked at the faces that greeted him. There were a lot of knowing looks among the officers, expressions of determination and apprehension, in different mixes. Most of the high-ranking officers were around thirty, Hannibal's own age. They had virtually been brought up together and some, like Maharbal, could look back on fifteen years of campaigning with the general, in a shared apprenticeship under his father and brother-in-law. Two were close family of Hannibal's – Mago, the general's youngest brother, and Hanno, the son of his elder sister. The middle brother, Hasdrubal Barca, was not even in Italy; he had been left behind to defend Iberia from Roman attacks.

Hannibal had addressed the army two days before, and had succeeded in making the men believe they could beat any Roman army thrown at them, even one almost twice as large. Maharbal was torn. Reason wanted to tell him that it wasn't possible. Yes, they had beaten huge armies in Iberia and in Gaul; but those had been, well, Iberians and Gauls. These were eight Roman legions. And yet, Hannibal's confidence had rubbed off on everyone. Maharbal, who knew Hannibal better than any of the other men present, including Mago, knew the assurance he displayed was not a show he was putting on for their benefit. If there was one thing he was certain of, it was that Hannibal would not knowingly lead his army to certain death.

"Any news?" Mago asked as Maharbal entered.

"Nothing yet. But if he wants us to come together again here, I suppose that means *he* thinks we'll fight."

Mago nodded as if that settled it. He wore a look of grim determination, glad that the wait would soon be over, to have something to do, to get this battle over with.

Gisgo, who would be in charge of the skirmishers, was plainly putting on a brave face to cover his fretfulness. Qarthalo, a noble-born Punic officer, who would command part of the Libyan élite today, looked more worried than Monomachos, who would command the other half.

The oldest men in the tent were Barmokar, Myrkan, and another Mago, council elders from Qart-hadasht who had accompanied Hannibal since the early days of the war. They were studying the detailed map of the surrounding lands on both banks of the river Aufidus with what they probably hoped

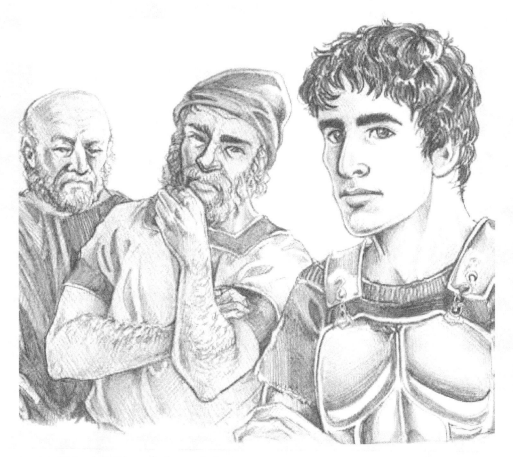

looked like level-headed capability.

Then there was Hanno, Hannibal's nephew, long a mainstay of his army though barely twenty-three; he would command the light Numidian cavalry and looked probably the most cheerfully confident of all the men assembled. With the possible exception of Hasdrubal. If you could ever call him cheerful.

Hasdrubal the Ugly was not, in fact, as ugly as his epithet implied, but having held a command under Hannibal's brother-in-law, Hasdrubal the Fair, a distinctive nickname had been required. What began as a joke had stuck, though Hasdrubal the Fair was now dead and Hasdrubal Barca remained in Iberia.

Today, he would command the heavy cavalry, looking as calm as ever at the prospect. Maharbal supposed that, once you had successfully got thirty-seven elephants across snow-covered mountains, there were few things in the world that would disconcert you. He, too, was studying the map, absently scratching his greying beard.

Every feature of the area had been drawn in; in addition, Hannibal probably knew every rock and blade of grass by name at this point. He must have spent thirty or forty hours out there over the past two weeks, studying every part of the terrain, the ground, the wind, and visibility on either side of the river, and thinking, usually alone. On the map lay wooden blocks representing the different tactical groups of both armies; an assortment of colours for the Punic, white for the Roman side.

"Left or right?" Hasdrubal asked Maharbal under his breath as he caught him watching. His tone was that of a man betting on contenders at a fist fight.

Maharbal didn't bat an eye. "Right."

"Really? He chose the left bank yesterday."

Maharbal winked. "Exactly."

They were interrupted by Hannibal entering the tent. The general's face was focused as he briskly moved to the map, fleetingly nodding at each of them by way of greeting. "Varro's flying the red *vexillum*," he said without preamble. "His skirmishers are on their way to the right bank of the river."

The reactions ranged from whistles to worried looks to stoic silence. Gisgo broke it. "So they have their way?"

"They *think* they have their way," Hannibal replied, exchanging a knowing look with Maharbal. "By deploying on the left bank yesterday, we've convinced them we don't want to fight on the right. Their scouts were roaming around there all yesterday afternoon. I can't say Varro's choice surprises me." Hannibal covered the wooden blocks with both hands, and with a sweeping gesture, moved them to the other bank. "In fact, we're prepared to fight wherever necessary."

There lay seven rectangular blocks for the Roman infantry line, with two small round ones for the cavalry at either side. Hannibal's centre consisted of seven smaller blocks, in different colours, two green, two red, three blue. At the flanks, there were two large round blocks for the cavalry, rather larger than the ones representing the Roman horse.

"True, we are giving up a small advantage for our cavalry if we have to fight on rougher ground," Hannibal went on, "but that's balanced by the fact that we'll have a lot more space for the Numidians on the right bank. They, on the other hand, are giving away a huge advantage for their largely untrained infantry. Either Varro is smart – and conservative – enough to keep his line close together, which enables us to envelope him on the wings. Or he's innovative – and dumb – enough to deploy in a long line to encircle us; in which case we're more likely to break through his centre as it bumbles along than he is to break through ours. None of the consuls – or, indeed, any Roman – has ever commanded an army of eighty-six thousand men. It must be a daunting experience for them. Under the circumstances, they will likely stick to any traditional setup they can. We'll see. If Varro indeed deploys in a long thin line, just remember what we said about breaking through yesterday. It'll be even easier here.

"For the moment, however, we'll assume he is smart and conservative, and the original plan remains the same as ever, in its main points." He positioned six of the seven Roman infantry rectangles as a neat, solid line with spaces be-tween the blocks in a line perpendicular to the river. "We'll assume they'll leave a garrison of about ten thousand to guard their camps. According to our spies, eight thousand are light infantry. Which leaves us about sixty-two thousand heavy infantry to deal with." He put down the last infantry block in the larger Roman camp, then looked at each of the men assembled in turn and went on, sombrely, "At the risk of boring you into a stupor, here are the details again. If you want to, sing along; it can't hurt."

"It will, if I do," Hasdrubal growled. Hanno chuckled; Mago snorted.

"Hanno," Hannibal addressed his nephew. "Take the Numidians and lead them across the river. If the Roman velites want to harass our skirmishers while they deploy, harass them back. Keep them in the north of the plain; they'll have the sun and the dust in their faces. And keep them clear of the hill where our first camp was." He pointed to a spot southeast of the wooden blocks. "I want that hill. I need to see what they're up to."

Hanno nodded. "Understood."

Hasdrubal kneaded his chin through his beard. "That leaves us a rather cramped area between the river, the Roman camp, and those hills."

"Yes," Hannibal agreed. "But we won't be able to force them to face the river. Not after the Trebia. Still, a cramped space also favours us, as they won't be able to fan out and encircle us."

He positioned a round cavalry block on the right flank of his infantry line, which was still in a jumble. "Hanno, you're going to take the right wing, to have maximum movement without the river getting in your way. Unless the Romans deviate from cherished tradition, you'll have the allied horse against you. Their strength still isn't up to scratch after the blows we've dealt them over the last two years. Your goal is to chase them off, though you may need Hasdrubal for that. More about that in a bit. Keep your men in hand. If you al-low them to pursue a fleeing enemy and leave our flank unprotected, we lose. Either a lot of lives, or a lot of lives and a battle. Even with the Roman cavalry gone, they'll still have enough reserves to outflank us with just their infantry.

Granted, it would take a fair bit of innovation on their part to consider it, let alone mobility they probably don't have, but we would be mad to just assume they wouldn't think of it. Clear?"

Hanno acknowledged. "Clear."

Hannibal turned to Hasdrubal. "So, on to the left wing."

The seasoned service corps officer gave a nod.

"You'll have to work with a deep formation and a short front," Hannibal

continued. "You will probably have the Roman citizen cavalry against you, almost certainly led by Varro, as the commanding officer. You'll outnumber them by a considerable margin, but they would be mad to give you much space. Work with what you have. I trust you there."

Hasdrubal nodded, watching as Hannibal placed the other cavalry block on the left flank, close to the river on the map.

"A lot depends on you," Hannibal said with emphasis. "They won't stand much of a chance against you, but they'll fight fiercely. As with Hanno, if – or rather, when – they break, do not expose our flank. Your ultimate goal is the same – expose the Roman flank and attack it. You two will have to coordinate your moves quite a bit as the battle progresses. Use the open space behind the lines for that. Once the fighting in the centre starts, chances are I won't be able to stay in contact with you."

Hannibal gnawed his lower lip. Maharbal knew that this was the part that the general was still not completely happy with. Hannibal had never given away so much control before, in a situation where so much could go wrong, through inattention, misjudgment, or plain bad luck. In the first discussions of the battle plans, with just the inner council – Hannibal, Hasdrubal, Mago, Hanno, and Maharbal – the general had intended to com-mand the heavy cavalry wing himself, until it had become apparent beyond a shadow of doubt that the centre was the glaringly weak point in the equation, and that the only thing that might stand a chance of enabling the centre to hold out long enough was Hannibal's presence. They had played through several alterna-tives – Libyans in the centre, Iberians at the flanks, but it had all boiled down to this. It had been at these mee-tings that it had been decided Maharbal would not be in su-preme command of the light cavalry.

"Maharbal will have an eye on the situation whenever he can spare one," Hannibal went on, looking at him directly. Maharbal still found the milky gaze of the general's blind right eye slightly disconcerting, though Hannibal often seemed to forget about the effect entirely. "You've all got fast riders on your sides; some communication ought to come through. I'm count-ing on your judgment."

Hasdrubal dipped his head solemnly. "All understood."

"Gisgo," Hannibal went on. "Hanno's Numidians will clear the way for the skirmishers. I want you to be in formation in one and a half hours at the very latest, so your men can screen the rest of our troops. We don't want Varro and Paullus to see what we're up to."

"Chances are they'll just be thoroughly confused if they do catch a glimpse," Maharbal remarked, to sniggers around the tent.

"Indeed, but I'm not going to take that chance." Hannibal chewed on his lip again. "At one point, *some* Roman commander is bound to get over manipular formations and understand something about tactics; Paullus and Varro aren't likely candidates, but still."

He turned to Monomachos and Qarthalo. "So, for the Libyans." He picked up the two green rectangles and placed them between the still-jumbled red and blue centre pieces and the cavalry, facing forward with their narrow side. "The two of you will be flanking Mago and me in the centre with five thousand Libyan hoplites each. You'll deploy them in deep formation, so they don't look like much from the front. You're our reserve if things go bad and the Romans break through, which, hopefully, Mago and I will prevent. As long as the centre holds, you stand where you are. I can't stress this enough. If the Romans force our centre, then, and only then are you to leave your posts and prevent a rout. If that happens, act on my signal only.

"But this is the worst case scenario. Rather than as backup, I need you to be the jaws of the trap. If you spring it too soon, you risk alerting the Romans to what we're up to.

"This brings us to the greatest dangers. The first is obvious and, literally, pressing. The Roman centre will comprise at least sixty thousand, and that is a careful estimate. They broke through our lines at the Trebia and at Trasimene, and we survived that because it wasn't a concerted action on their part, and all they wanted to do was get clear. At Trebia and Trasimene, they didn't reform and just ran. We won't have that today." He looked up from the battle plan, his face serious. "Yesterday, I heard from captives that the Roman tribunes have made every man swear a holy vow not to abandon their arms or flee, on pain of death. This is far from uncommon, but the oath is new. They take these things seriously; there won't be much surrender. Pass that on to the commanders."

He pointed out the cavalry units at either flank, on either side. "Cavalry, as ever, is their weakness. They know they can't win on the wings, so they'll try to crush our centre with their sheer numbers. Brute strength instead of

finesse. Not that they were ever notorious for the latter." This time, nobody laughed. "But it's their best hope, and they're bound to know that, too. We'll deny our centre as long as we can, until our wings have secured the battle for us."

He picked up the last of the pieces, two red and three blue rectangles for the Spanish and Celtic infantry, and laid them, alternatingly, across the centre. The only way he could make them stretch all the way between the two green blocks representing the Libyans was by laying them down with their wider sides to the front, which starkly revealed how thin they were.

"Mago and I will command in the centre. Compared to the rest of you, our task is straightforward – a slow and orderly retreat. The junior officers have all been instructed to prevent heroic advances, and frantic backward scrambles."

He did not need to remind them all that especially the Celts were notorious for both.

Hannibal caught Mago's grimace. "I know. We have roughly sixty thousand eager Romans who want to break through our twenty-four thousand Iberians and Gauls. And who wouldn't say no to our heads served on a silver platter either. We just have to make sure they don't get any of that. Instead, we can use their eagerness against them. If they see us retreat-ing, they'll push on, and won't see the Libyans at their flanks until it's too late."

"What if they smell the trap before that?" the oldest of the councillors, Myrkan, asked. "If they refuse to be baited at all?"

"Makes no difference, on the whole," Hannibal said. "If they won't come at us, we'll come at them. I'd actually prefer that, as it would give us more control and doesn't force us onto the defensive. But don't expect that to happen. They want revenge for Trasimene. And it's a trap that is almost impossible to smell. Certainly not for an army that has been using the same tactics for a couple of centuries and doesn't regroup or reform as circumstances demand it."

He turned to Maharbal. "The other crucial point is timing. So far, our timing has usually been flawless, but for today, we will have to step it up yet another notch. We've never been up against anything as insanely huge as this Roman army, and this battle is bound to be long and, even in the best of circumstances, messy. Timing has never been this vital. The smallest misjudgment can ruin everything, literally everything. Maharbal, that's why I'm leaving you without a direct command, to be my eyes and ears on the field."

Maharbal nodded, biting back an eye-related remark. Usually, Hannibal took them in stride, but he had to concede this was hardly the moment.

"Changes in the Roman line; our cavalry actions; and, most importantly and hopefully unnecessarily, breakthroughs in our centre," Hannibal went on, counting them off on his fingers. "If anything unforeseen happens, try to get word through to me, but act on your own initiative if you don't hear back from me. Or can't reasonably expect to hear back from me. If anything unexpected happens, or an opportunity presents itself that we haven't considered, make use of every unit that's available."

Maharbal nodded again. "You can count on me."

Hannibal turned to the council elders. "Myrkan, Barmokar, Mago, I'll ask you to see to the necessary sacrifices and rites and assure the men of our divine assistance. The rest of you, prepare to march out your troops. Every man is to eat enough breakfast, fill water flasks, and arm himself. We have a long day ahead of us."

He straightened to look at each of them in turn and spread his hands. "My friends – together, we have beaten three consular armies. Today, we're facing the equivalent of four. A few of you have asked me over the past few days, sometimes in less plain words, why I wasn't worried. I'll tell you why – because I know I can completely rely on you. If the gods offered me to trade – eighty-six thousand largely untrained men and mediocre officers for fifty thousand of the best fighters in the world, and a handful of the best officers that any general has ever had – I know what I would choose."

Cornelius Lentulus had rid himself of the toga he had worn while he was taking the auspices; now, he wore a sashed bronze cuirass, cloak, and Corinthian helmet, the signs of his military rank.

The look on Paullus' face as he had mentioned the auspices had left him with a leaden feeling in his stomach. It hadn't been his intention to slight Paullus of a victory. As a matter of fact, his original intent had been to leave the chickens hungry so they would eat yesterday, but he was slowly starting to understand that chickens' appetites were indeed a matter of supernatural provenance, especially with two consuls breathing down your neck.

Centurions were shouting orders in Paullus' camp, as legionaries and allies, armed for battle, readied themselves to form up and march out, to take up position on the field to the south. Lentulus saw two of his fellow tribunes nearly coming to blows over which of them would lead out his units first. Regular order was upset with the presence of so many legions and the distribution over two camps.

Lentulus had already assembled his three *turmae* of riders, ninety in all, led by three decurions, and was on his way to the eastern gate. As he had surmised, the decurions had grumbled when he had told them to assemble their men and accompany him on a scouting mission, but even though he fully shared their sentiments, he was determined not to let it show.

Lentulus led his three *turmae* around the eastern part of the field in a wide sweep, looking out for any spots where the Carthaginian might have hidden an ambush. He quickly felt certain that there was nothing in a radius of two or three miles that they would not see. The ground was dry and dusty, a few solitary ears of barley or wild wheat jutting up in places. The crops had long been harvested – not by the Apulian farmers that had sown them, but by Hannibal's army. Here and there, a patch of half-withered wild poppy stood out, blood-red in the pale yellow.

The sun had now risen, and there was not a cloud in the sky; the day promised to be hot and sunny. Overhead, swarms of crows were circling, attracted by the remains of corn left by the Carthaginians, and three camps full of people producing waste. For Lentulus, ignoring the ominous black birds took a great amount of willpower.

"Finest battle-weather!" The voice of Manlius, one of the decurions, interrupted his thoughts. "Better than ever. I've been at the Trebia. Jupiter Optimus Maximus, I haven't been so cold in my life. Or ever again. I'll take the

Apulian sun any day."

"Might use some of that snow and sleet here today," one of the decurion's riders remarked. "It's going to be a long, hot day."

"Hot, maybe," replied Manlius. "But not long. If we're lucky, the fighting will be over before the afternoon heat. If the Carthaginian even comes out. He'd be mad to, but well, we know that he is."

Lentulus turned in the saddle, to look at the decurion. "You were at the Trebia?" he asked. "What was the terrain like?"

Manlius gave a derisive snort. "Terrain? We hardly saw any terrain. Those of us who weren't freezing our balls off and had any eyes for our surroundings saw only snow and elephants. Let's praise the gods that we killed all of those. Though even Hannibal'd have a job hiding elephants." His men laughed.

"Elephants, maybe," Lentulus said. "But he wasn't hiding those. What sort of place did he hide his ambush in, at the Trebia? Did you see that?"

"I wouldn't be here if I had," Manlius grumbled. "The ambush hit the left flank. But there would have been loads of places at the riverbank, with the snow and bushes and everything."

"Let's get closer to the river," Lentulus said. "If there is a place where... the Carthaginian might hide something, we will find it." Why was it so difficult to say the enemy's name? It had become a habit in the entire army to refer to him mainly as "the Carthaginian", even though that was twice as long as the name – as though the name was an evil spell that might somehow conjure him out of nowhere. Varro remained one of the few people Lentulus knew who frequently referred to the enemy by his name. It made him flinch every time, despite himself. The man was on his way to become a story to scare children with.

The Aufidus glistened lazily in the early morning sun as Lentulus and his men approached. The men were becoming more and more uneasy the nearer they came to the river. A while ago, all of them had deemed an ambush ludicrous; now, with stories of the Trebia and seeing the overgrown bank before them, across which they knew lay the enemy camp, they suddenly weren't so sure.

They rode upriver, looking for any signs of the enemy. Once, one of the men cast a spear into a patch of high yellow reeds when they heard a rustle, and out dashed something small on four legs, and raced off, up the river.

"A fox!" one of the men exclaimed. A few laughed at the fright in his tone, but more looked worriedly at Lentulus, waiting for the augur to explain what it meant.

"That means nothing!" Lentulus tried to calm them. "It was a fox on a riverbank. There is nothing unusual about it. You, retrieve your spear. The rest of you, we're riding back downriver. If the Carthaginian has hidden any men, it won't be this far from the battlefield."

"If anything, the fox is a good sign, isn't it?" asked Manlius. "Think – it wouldn't be here if there were a bunch of armed men waiting in ambush just a few yards away!"

They had ridden half a mile and were passing another patch of thick shrubs which obscured the river and the other bank, when the decurion of the ninth *turma*, who was ahead of the rest, suddenly pulled up sharply.

"Not another fox?" laughed Manlius. His laugh turned into a gurgle as a

spear came hurtling from beyond the rushes and pierced his throat. His horse shied and reared, throwing him off and bolting.

"Back!" Lentulus shouted. "Back!" he repeated, even louder, as the decurion of the ninth was about to lead a charge into the rushes. "We have no idea how many they are!"

He waited for barely a heartbeat to see if his command was obeyed; as soon as he saw his men turning their horses, he followed suit, racing away from the river. More spears were flying. He heard shouts from behind them, too, in a language he didn't understand.

"Numidians!" one of his men yelled. "Curse them!"

"An ambush!" another shouted.

They were breaking from the rushes now. Twenty, forty – Lentulus considered ordering his men to turn and fight, and retrieve Manlius' body – then he looked over his shoulder again, and he could see a greater force of the lightly armed men on their small, fast horses, gathering on the other bank.

"Tribune!" one of the decurions shouted at him. "We can't just run! Let's at least send them one volley of spears!"

"Too many," Lentulus panted. "Paullus wants news, not dead heroes."

"It was an ambush!" another of the riders was still shouting.

"It was *not*!" Lentulus replied, crossly. "That was the whole damn Numidian cavalry."

When he turned in the saddle again, he saw with relief that they were not being followed. It seemed the Numidians had been just as surprised as they had been, and had deemed them too unimportant a target to waste energy on, or more spears.

Finally, he had his troop slow down to a trot, and looked back again. Most of the enemy light cavalry had crossed the river. Further northeast, the skirmishers were moving out. Lentulus' heart was beating in his throat. His day of battle had already brought tampered-with auspices, a fox, and flight. You didn't have to be an augur to know that none of these were good omens.

Hannibal rode up the hill he had ordered Hanno to keep from the Romans, accompanied by Maharbal, a dozen dispatch riders, and the five men of his guard. Bomilkar was riding at his right; the guard captain was left-handed, which made him the perfect man for that position. Additionally, after the loss of his right eye, Hannibal was especially vulnerable to anything coming in from that side in the midst of battle, and he was glad to have someone there on whom he could completely rely. Two of the other men were Libyans, the other two Iberians, distant relatives of his wife.

Hanno was awaiting them with a contingent of fifty Numidians; the men, bare-headed and barefoot, clad only in their light tunics and protected by round shields, sat on the equally bare backs of their unbridled horses, controlling them only by a braided strap round the neck.

The hill-top was covered with grass and wild corn, growing around broken stones of older Italic ruins that jutted out among them. Cannae wasn't much. A ruined citadel, and a Roman granary; now his.

"Anything unusual?" Hannibal asked Hanno.

"Yes and no," his nephew replied. "The first unit of my men encountered a troop of Roman scouts as they crossed the river. Less than a hundred. I called my men back when they wanted to pursue."

"Good work, Hanno. Casualties?"

"One. Roman."

"The first blood of the day," Maharbal murmured. "They've taken up scouting now, have they? That's cute. What's next? Ambushes?"

"Too distinctly un-Roman," Hannibal said, patting his horse's neck. He was armoured for battle; in linen cuirass, greaves, a simple Thracian helmet and a similarly unadorned shield, he looked little different from the other Punic officers. Hannibal would very likely find himself in the thick of battle as the day wore on; his men would recognise him, and take courage from seeing their general fighting alongside them, but the Romans would not be able to pick him out easily among his guard and the other commanders. Still, Bomilkar was not a man to be envied today.

Ten stades to the north, the Roman battle line was assembling, just south of the smaller Roman camp. Hannibal knew that it could take until noon before both battle lines were ready, possibly longer. Hannibal's troops had had breakfast and filled flasks with water, unhurriedly moving out to deploy. Their train-ing from ten or twenty years of campaigning – some going back to his father Hamilkar – was easily apparent as they fell into their positions without effort. Even the Celts, who had been following his standard for just one and a half years, had shaped up remarkably. Eight thousand of his troops, mainly Gauls, with a few Iberians and Gaetulans, would remain behind to guard the camp. Mago had objected to leaving so many men behind "with their thumbs in their ears", but Hannibal had been adamant. He could do without them, though with difficulty. But to lose the camp, and their baggage, would be a great blow, as he was sure the Romans knew, too.

His cavalry, the pride of his army, were already in their positions at the flanks of the Punic skirmishers; dust was swirling up under the restless hooves of four thousand Numidian and six thousand Celtic and Iberian horses. The Volturnus wind was blowing it across the field to the north-east.

"It's going to be hard to see much of the Romans from here," Maharbal remarked, shielding his eyes with his hand.

"It's going to be hard for the Romans to see much of anything." Hannibal rubbed his right eye; an old habit. "Hasdrubal needs to move closer to the river," he said, grimacing. "He won't like it a bit, but he's taking up too much space there. If he stays like that, we'll have the Roman centre overlapping ours."

Hanno looked at his uncle. "Shall I ride down and tell him?"

"Yes, see to it. If he doesn't like it, tell him to bite off *my* head, if he dares; not yours."

Hanno grinned. "I'll tell him." He whistled on two fingers; his riders turned their mounts and rode after him.

Hannibal signalled the guards to stay behind and dismounted, climbing up a short distance further, to the highest outcropping. Maharbal followed.

Hannibal stood and watched the Roman centre. "So, Varro is smart and conservative. He's not even trying to fan out his line to span further than ours."

Maharbal nodded. "So it seems." He shook his head at seeing the masses of legionaries marching up. "We've only ever seen such numbers among Spanish tribes, who don't even bother to try and march in formation, haven't we? Gods above and below, commanding and *feeding* that thing has to be a nightmare."

Hannibal gave a humourless laugh. "You remember the last time I had that many? I sent a few thousand home as soon as they gave me half a reason."

Maharbal cast him a sidelong glance. "You are still sure that we will win this."

Hannibal did not answer at once. "I know we *can* win this."

Had he given any thought to the possibility of losing? Over the past weeks, he had pushed that thought from his mind, as it wasn't about to help him. But of course it had come, unbidden, rearing its ugly head every now and then. He had not shared it with anyone, at least not in words; there had been no need for it, it had been omnipresent, always there, always under the surface, beaten into submission with cool reason and a fair portion of bravado, un-voiced, so as not to call bad luck on them.

Hannibal had not forgotten the Alps, that outrageous endeavour that made up more than half of his reputation, on the Roman side of this war as well as on his own. The losses had been staggering. Though he had felt certain, befo-

re the fact, that he had done all in his power to get his men – or most of them – to the other side, it hadn't been enough. His reputation had not suffered, or if it had, it had quickly recovered; but there was still the dread that there was something glaring, something fatal, that he had left out of his calculations. Something that would open up the ground under him and tear everything down in its wake. This was a dread he had never confided to anyone, not even Mago, though he suspected that Maharbal had caught glimpses of it over time, though he had never commented on it. The Alps had been a harsh lesson that must never be repeated.

Now, he had found some comfort in the knowledge that by tonight, one way or the other, this war was likely to be over. If Rome lost eight legions – or four or five of them – there was no way this would not break her. And if he lost, the only thing he asked of the gods was to die today in the knowledge that he had done all that was humanly possible to prevent defeat.

Across the field, something unusual in the Roman deployment pattern suddenly made Hannibal squint. The gaps between the individual maniples were receding, blocks of legionaries moving closer together, or so it appeared to him, but he could be mistaken. Since the fever that had cost him the sight of his right eye, over a year ago now, he had been forced to accept that his eyesight as a whole had suffered. "Maharbal," he said. "Look at those maniples of the main Roman infantry and tell me what they're doing."

Maharbal took his time, stared, blinked, rubbed his eyes. "If I didn't know better," he said slowly, "I would say they are abandoning manipular tactics."

"They're massing together, yes?"

Maharbal blinked again. "Yes. Packed tightly."

For a moment, Hannibal stood silently, drumming the fingers of his right hand against his left elbow, staring at the now-indistinguishable mass of legionaries, unable to believe what he saw. Whether Varro was unable to get his untrained men to stay in their usual square-tile formation, or whether he was doing it on purpose to present an even stronger centre, it surpassed his wildest dreams. His mouth felt dry as, in his mind, white wooden blocks merged into a tight, dense mass, as he saw the incredible possibility. All the incredible possibilities.

"So we can shorten our front as well, reinforce our centre, have more reserves," Maharbal observed.

"We might... we might." Hannibal closed his eyes, still saw the shapes in his mind's eye, watched as they moved. He might shorten his line... or he might do something completely new.

"Do you remember the ambush at Searo?" Hannibal finally asked, his eyes still closed.

Maharbal had been seventeen, Hannibal fifteen, when the Iberian Oretani tribe had caught their small cavalry unit by surprise in a narrow ravine. If Hamilkar hadn't turned up with a larger contingent of cavalry just in time, neither of them would be standing here today. "Hardly, thanks to the rock to the head I took early into the fighting," Maharbal replied. "You'll never stop reminding me, will you?"

Hannibal didn't smile. "It was more the mechanics of the ambush. Surrounded on all sides, all exits blocked – the Oretani had made sure we couldn't move. I've seen it in action – men packed tight, with nowhere to go. Soldiers becoming little more than frightened cattle. We saw a fraction of that at Trasimene, but there was still more space overall. More than here..." His voice trailed off, his thoughts racing.

"*Surrounded on all sides?*" Maharbal echoed, one eyebrow creeping towards his hairline.

"It can be done," Hannibal breathed, slowly opening his eyes again. Everything suddenly looked cool, clear, cut. "Massed this tightly, we could draw the ring all around them."

Maharbal shook his head vehemently. "We were, what, three hundred men? This is a bloody seventy thousand we're talking about. Complete encirclement? Against such a huge army? That's madness."

Hannibal barely heard him, shaking his head as if to fend off a fly, not taking his eye off the Roman line. "It doesn't matter. The mechanics are the same. Seventy thousand might be even worse. One man loses his footing, five others stumble, then twenty-five, then a hundred and twenty-five... pandemonium. It's simple mathematics. The length of our Iberian and Celtic infantry matches theirs... and on top of that, we'd have..." He exhaled sharply, became aware of his drumming fingertips, and forcibly stopped himself. He could see it with his eyes open now, the perfect encirclement, a trap from which there would be no escape. If he could make this work, if he could only make this work... The gods were laying everything in his grasp. He need only take it, and

hold on. It could be done.

Maharbal was watching him. He must have recognised the look on the general's face; Hannibal must have had it at other times, at the Rhone, at the Trebia, and very probably at Trasimene. This must be how a hawk felt looking at a fat, unsuspecting rabbit. And then, there was the fear the hawk probably didn't know, following only his instinct; the gut-wrenching fear of Tantalos seeing the juicy fruits within his reach only to be swept aside by a vengeful breeze. The wild instinct of the beast and the reasoning of man which was guided by logic and fear. He knew he would need both today, in exactly the right measure. If fear was channelled in the right way, it could be forced into logic.

"The Oretani had solid walls of rock," Maharbal pointed out. "We'll have, what? A few lines of armed men – stretched very thin. It seems a stretch to just equate the two. Especially with the Romans turning themselves into a fucking battering ram."

A predatory smile crept over Hannibal's face. "Exactly, Maharbal. How do you counter a battering ram?"

"I don't know. Set it on fire?"

Hannibal's grin grew wider. "Open the door."

Maharbal shook his head. "That doesn't make a bit of sense."

Hannibal winked. "Don't blame me for expanding the metaphor – you brought it up. We don't *want* to keep out the battering ram. And we're not an immovable door either. What we want is to get it inside the walls with our door intact to slam it shut. If the battering ram encounters no door, all the force behind will just come to nothing." He unconsciously resumed his drumming. "Greed," he said, half to himself. "We need to draw them in by their greed. If they think they're winning, and then realise they're surrounded – a man's psyche can't deal with that." He turned, and called to one of his dispatch riders, who were waiting fifteen feet away. "Iuba, find Hasdrubal. Now. He's to join me in the centre."

The rider dashed off.

"And tomorrow? March on Rome?" Maharbal said, only half in jest.

Hannibal shook his head, still barely paying attention. "If... this works out... I'd rather they came to us. With olive branches."

"They're more likely to stick them in your back than to sue for peace."

"I rather hope that, after today, they'll be glad when we accept."

"I pray to the gods that you're right," said Maharbal, so low that the bodyguard didn't hear.

Hannibal shook himself, clapped his friend's shoulder. "And the Romans will pray to theirs that I'm not. In some cases, we're praying to the same ones. Who can say on what whims they decide whom to listen to, and to whom to close their ears?" He felt feverish as he climbed down the craggy hillside. He needed to ride down, make adjustments to the infantry line.

Bomilkar held Hannibal's horse by the bridle as the general mounted. He turned to Maharbal.

"Stay on the lookout up here. Send a rider if anything changes."

Maharbal gave a solemn nod, patting his horse's rump. "In case I don't see you again until – afterwards..." His voice trailed off, and he touched three fingers to his chest, for luck.

"Yes. You, too."

"Let him try any of his Punic treachery *here*."

Terentius Varro stood on a small hillock at the south entrance of the Roman camp on the right bank of the river, rubbing dust from his eyes as he watched the armies forming up for battle on the open plain of Cannae, his staff beside him. The largest army Rome had ever fielded. Eight legions, and the corresponding numbers of Italian allies.

The ground might be rocky, but they had made sure to meet Hannibal on the plainest stretch of land in all of Italy. There was no way the Carthaginian could have hidden any surprise attacks here, unless his ambush troops were the size of field mice. Without any of his tricks, on the open plain, even his cavalry would not save him. The river would protect the right Roman flank, the hills the left.

Varro was no fool; he knew that the enemy's cavalry superiority would cause losses. But in the end, it would break and flee when the legions broke the centre.

Varro's only half-worry was for his victory to be marred by Hannibal escaping, or being killed. What wouldn't he give for the Carthaginian in his triumphal procession, alive and in fetters.

Beside Varro stood his colleague Paullus, his expression unreadable. How Paullus would loathe it when Varro, a plebeian, emerged victorious over Hannibal. The gods had denied Paullus his stab at glory yesterday; today, glory would be Varro's.

Next to the consuls were the other two legates; Servilius Geminus, last year's consul, and Minucius Rufus.

Servilius had never faced Hannibal in an open battle himself, but he had lost four thousand horse to him the previous year, which he had sent to the aid of his colleague Flaminius, not knowing that he had already run into Hannibal's trap at Lake Trasimene. His four thousand had soon shared the fate of Flaminius' legions. Servilius, too, was intent on making amends.

Minucius Rufus was the only one of the senior Roman officers who could boast about having survived a small-scale battle against the Carthaginian, and was eager to finally see him beaten. Last year, he had served as Master of Horse to Fabius Maximus, the dictator who had decreed that meeting Hannibal in battle meant certain defeat. For six months, the senate had accepted that. But even Fabius had to know that wars were not won by thumb-twiddling.

At the break of dawn, they had heard the trumpets from the Carthaginian camp, and had known their challenge had been accepted. Now, Hannibal's Numidians were beating up dust as they swept over the plain, shielding his skirmishers as they deployed in a long line, in turn shielding his infantry. Varro's own army, too, was getting into position.

The spectacle, he had to concede, was hardly as imposing as it ought to have been; especially the junior legionaries – *velites* and *hastati* – having trouble staying in their formations. Varro shook his head impatiently. It didn't matter. Once they were in formation, the sheer mass of them, and their centurions, would keep them in line. The men, every last of them, were eager to finally put the war in Italy to an end. They all knew what was at stake.

"Tonight, Hannibal's army will be no more," Varro said. "And without him, the war in Iberia will turn quickly."

Aemilius Paullus nodded slowly. "We've got a fair part of his cavalry pinned against the river, and we're outnumbering his infantry two to one. I don't see

how he can hope to win this. The scouts I sent out earlier today haven't found any signs of an ambush." He sounded as if he still had to convince himself of it.

With a sour expression, Servilius was watching a dust cloud moving around the enemy lines to the flank; in it, horses were visible, in a loose oblong formation. "What's he doing now – deploying his whole Numidian cavalry on his right wing?"

Varro squinted. On their left, the Carthaginian right wing indeed appeared to consist of solely light cavalry. He could feel his stomach drop. This was something he had not anticipated. They had always assumed that Hannibal would split his heavy cavalry between his wings, and let his Numidians attack in small groups all across the field, as he had done at the Trebia. It was part of the reason why Varro had ordered a tight formation, to present shield walls to scattered enemy attacks. For a moment, he was tempted to correct that, but that would take hours – in which Hannibal might attack before the lines stood once more. That was the downside to the largest army Rome had ever fielded – relaying orders seemed to take disproportionally long.

They just had to hold out, he told himself. The battle on the wings would be tough, but it wouldn't be for long. Nothing would withstand his legions in the centre.

"Didn't he usually treat the Numidians as... mounted skirmishers?" Minucius asked uneasily.

Servilius spat. "Can we really say what he *usually* does?" he said bitterly. "He's used them as flank protection at Ticinus, as skirmishers at the Trebia, to block the exits at Trasimene..."

"... and as an advance guard against you," Varro said pointedly. "But here's another good omen. There's nothing around for miles that starts with a *T*."

"So, whatever 'usual' is for Hannibal, he seems to plan on using his Numidians as regular cavalry today," Paullus observed.

Servilius voiced what the consul had left unsaid. "And throws his entire heavy cavalry against our right wing. We will be heavily outmatched there." He shot Paullus a sidelong glance.

Paullus set his jaw. "Gallic riff-raff against Roman knights. Every one of ours is worth three of theirs. We're as evenly matched as we can hope to be."

Servilius grimaced. "And if we reinforced the right wing with ten maniples or so?"

Varro shook his head emphatically. "That would cause more confusion than support. The men wouldn't know their place in formation. No, that's not feasible." He inwardly cursed the Carthaginian. Who had ever heard of anyone whose army consisted of one-fifth cavalry, and who never used his units in the same way twice? How to counter such a ridiculous setup? How on earth did Hannibal's soldiers not get confused? "No, we will fight as we always have. Our procedure should be clear. It doesn't befit us to try and match him in his trickery. Fifty years ago, the Carthaginians forced us to fight on sea; we forced them to fight as if on land, and won. Now, Hannibal would force us to fight in cavalry battles; we will force upon him our infantry battle. Plain and simple."

"There is no way he will withstand our numbers," said Minucius with emphasis. "His infantry will shatter before he can make much use of his cavalry.

What will he do? His bag of tricks is empty. He's made us paranoid. Gods above, we'll finally be able to stop worrying tonight. This has been going on for far too long."

"Minucius is right, " Paullus said. "Eighteen months of being played for fools has made us edgy. But let us not forget he has never beaten us in open battle except by deceit. It's time we broke this curse."

"Two weeks from now, we'll enter Rome in triumph," Varro agreed. "Now, take your positions. Paullus, as agreed, the citizen cavalry." The victory would be his already; he could afford to be generous by giving Paullus the more prestigious command. "Rufus, Geminus, to the centre." He then looked around to the tribunes standing behind, signalling to four of them. "Octavius, Scipio, Publicius, Piso – come with me."

Three of them turned to accompany the consul to his command post on the left wing, with the allied cavalry; the fourth stood squinting, spell-bound, at the battle lines.

"Scipio."

Publius Cornelius Scipio didn't take his eyes off the plain. "What's he doing with his centre?" the young man said. "It looks... dented."

Piso and Octavius laughed. Varro turned towards the south, having to squint now that the sun was rising higher. Barely visible in the dust behind the skirmishers' lines, Hannibal's infantry line did indeed look uneven, in a strangely symmetrical way, but it was hard to discern much.

"The dog doing his tricks," the consul said with contempt. "It's probably just his reserve he's keeping back. He'll have to use it soon enough. Do you see how thin his line is?" He clapped young Scipio's shoulder. "Here's an idea – he'll be our prisoner tonight. Then you can ask him all about tactics. And dented centres."

Hannibal made his way along the line of mixed Iberian and Celtic contingents. Every now and then, he would single out a junior officer, beckoning at them to follow him.

He found Mago bellowing orders, to even out the line of alternating Iberians and Celts; the Celts, most of them bare-chested and eager to meet the Romans, were not known for their patience in holding formation.

Hannibal grasped Mago's shoulder. "Mago, listen," he shouted over the noise of thousands of men finding their places in formation. "Slight change of plan." He saw that the messenger he'd sent for Gisgo had returned, and swung from the saddle. He squatted on the ground, casting around for a stick and then drawing his dagger when he found only broken stalks of corn. Mago, bewildered, stared

at him from horseback, before he, too, dismounted and squatted down. Gisgo and the junior officers followed suit. Hannibal could tell that they were all just as bewildered, but determined not to let it show.

With the dagger, Hannibal quickly drew the Roman battle lines into the already trampled, dry yellow earth and added the river line. "The Romans are massing their lines deeply together, with the spaces between the maniples reduced," he quickly explained to them. "That opens up a chance we need to take." He drew in his own cavalry, the two columns of Libyans. "Our centre is too long now. We *might* correct that by deepening it. But we won't. Instead of positioning our centre in a straight line," he drew it faintly, then immediately wiped it out again, "I want us to do this." With the dagger point, he scraped a crescent into the ground, its bulge towards the Romans. Then he looked at

Mago. "Do you see it?"

Mago stared at the highly unconventional form in the sand. With a sinking feeling, Hannibal realised that Mago didn't see it. His brother was fiercely loyal, an able leader, a formidable fighter and a reliable recipient of orders, but he had never been able to grasp his brother's tactical ideas as quickly as Maharbal, or their middle brother, Hasdrubal, who was now commanding the armies in Iberia. Maharbal had once joked that, when tactical genius had been dealt out among Hamilkar's sons, Hannibal had grabbed the lion's share, and Hasdrubal had scooped up almost everything that was left. He had made sure never to tell Mago that. He was yet young; he would shape up.

"Isn't that the reverse of the original plan?" Mago cautiously asked. "Instead of slowly retreating, you...?"

"No, no, no," Hannibal said emphatically. "Nothing changes. We still retreat, and draw them in. We're just starting from a different point, slimming down the actual fighting zone." He looked at the other officers, pointing the dagger at the foremost curve. "Less frontage. Fewer losses in the early stages. More opportunities to reinforce the fighting front. More time for the cavalry."

A few slow nods around him.

"So, the Romans push in," Hannibal went on, impatiently. "We retreat. Our crescent flattens out – like this – and finally bends the other way." He demonstrated this on the ground. "The Romans will not be able to mimic these manoeuvres; even if they saw through it, and had the training, they wouldn't have the space. We'll throw them into disorder, but *they'll* think that *we're* breaking, and won't even think it necessary to reform. The crescent shape will enable us to keep much of the heavy infantry out of the fighting for slightly longer, buying us precious time. When they see us advancing, they'll press more tightly together in the centre, effectively neutralising themselves. If you will, the Romans are the fish – our crescent is the bait. We'll take out a large part of their centre without a single blow. Do you see it now?"

It would not be quite such an easy matter, but for now, the important thing was for everybody to understand it, and obey the orders accordingly. Hannibal quickly repeated the most important points in Iberian, to make sure the two Iberian officers in their number understood the major details. He waited until all the heads around him were nodding, a few still a little wide-eyed. He hoped that, with the aid of visuals in the sand, they had all understood his purpose, if not all of his words.

"Mago and I will take our units to the foremost part of the crescent," Hannibal said, straightening. Time was pressing now; but it was not too late to put the new manoeuvres into action. If all else failed, and the Romans sounded the attack before his crescent stood, he could still work with an in-between solution. "Alco, Mutumbal, you have the middle position on your respective wings. Make sure you end up level with each other. After Mago and me, your task will be the trickiest – to make sure our line bends the right way and *does not break*. I remember the way you kept your men together when you led our right flank across the Tagos five years ago, under enemy attack, and still in good order. If I can trust anyone with this, it's you."

The Iberian and the Libyphoenician nodded solemnly, with quite a bit of pride.

"Bodeshmun, Sedaca, you have the positions furthest back; the two horns of the crescent, as it were, closest to the Libyans. Pass it down to your units." Dismissed, the officers mounted their horses again and rode back to their positions to carry out Hannibal's orders.

"Iltaces, Medesh," Hannibal addressed two of the dispatch riders in his staff. "You heard what this was all about?"

The men came forward and acknowledged.

"Iltaces," Hannibal said in Iberian. "Can you relay this to Maharbal?"

The Iberian dipped his head. "Yes. Half-moon facing forward, slimmer fighting zone, half-moon flattening, then facing the other way. Romans drawn in and thrown into disorder."

"Great man. You'll find him on the hill up by the old citadel. See to it."

Iltaces raced off. Hannibal made sure Medesh would also be able to relay the change of plans, and sent him to Hanno, then rode along the line to the Libyan columns at the flanks to instruct Monomachos and Qarthalo in person, with explicit orders that their part of the plan would not change one iota.

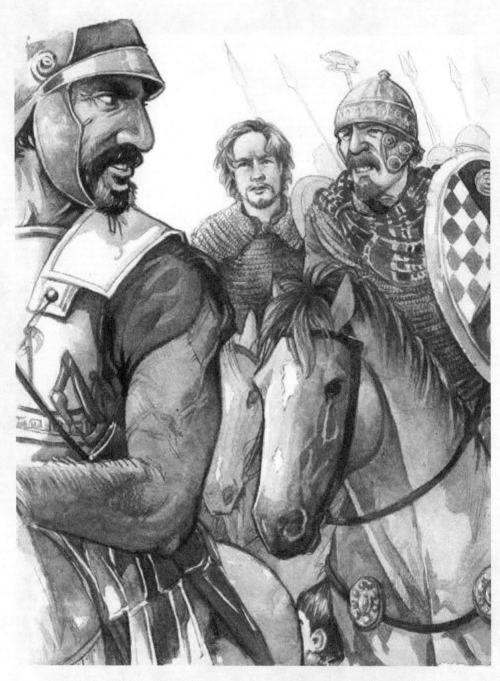

"So, every one of you, you're going to keep your squadrons together. There will be no pursuit unless I say so." Hasdrubal waited for his translators to repeat his words in Celtic and Iberian. For what would likely be the first of a dozen times today, he cursed inwardly at the need to rely on translators for his cavalry to understand orders in detail. To make things even more bizarre, he was speaking Greek; there were enough people in Hannibal's army who spoke Greek and Iberian, *or* Greek and Celtic, *or* Punic and Greek, *or* Punic and Iberian. Punic and Celtic was by far the most uncommon combination. "Our entire battle plan relies on seamless cooperation between the wings. Charging off on your own will not be tolerated."

Of course, for some of the officers under his command, he could have spoken Egyptian for all they cared about orders of this kind. He knew all that, of course. It was part of their culture. And he was the one who had been chosen to deal with this cultural mess, because he was such a caring and understanding soul.

Predictably, one of the Celtic chieftains – Hasdrubal searched his memory for the name; it was connected with previous run-ins of a similar kind – opened his mouth immediately and voiced strong objections, which Hasdrubal would have understood even without getting a single word. He actually did get one word – *barrus*, "heads".

Gabrannos, that was him.

Culture be damned.

"Tell him if he lets his people cut off heads for their collection, I will cut off their heads for *my* collection," he told the translator, a Ligurian Gaul. "*After* Hannibal is done with them. That means that their heads will look even uglier than usual. That's not a problem for me at all. I've been told that Punics have a taste for extremely ugly decorations."

The Ligurian looked at him, dumbfounded, not making any indication of translating. A few of the Iberian and Punic officers who understood some Greek stifled laughs. Gabrannos, realizing they were laughing about him, reddened in fury.

With a curse, Hasdrubal brought his horse close to that of Gabrannos. "You, take Rome-*barrus*," he hissed in all the Gallic he could muster, his face inches from that of the chieftain, "I, take your *barrus*."

He was aware that this had been a grammatical nightmare. That was fine with him. As long as it got the point across.

"You're in Hannibal's army," Hasdrubal growled, in Greek again, when Gabrannos remained silent. "Not in Gaul. When you swore allegiance to him, you also swore to follow his orders, and you will now follow mine. Is that understood?"

The Ligurian finished translating. Gabrannos glowered at Hasdrubal for a few more heartbeats before he dipped his head.

The Celtic chieftains were always a handful to keep in line, much more so than their foot soldiers. Those would listen to their chieftains, but they would also listen to their Punic officers, after a flogging at the very least. You couldn't flog the chieftains. Hannibal's army was a complicated body of levies and mercenaries, alliances and allegiances, the hope for loot or for glory or for both, and each of the officers was constantly treading a very fine line dealing with the different elements. Rome could draft; Hannibal was far from home and had to gain – and keep – support.

"Hasdrubal." Iuba, a Numidian dispatch rider, had approached from behind him. "The general wants to see you. He's in the centre."

Hasdrubal nodded. "I'm coming." He called to one of the Iberian chieftains whom he could trust to keep the men in hand (and find a few more fitting words about the taking of heads) to take over, and followed Iuba.

He found Hannibal not far from the left wing, with Qarthalo and his Libyans. The general was talking about a condensed Roman centre, and a plan to counter it by drawing out his own infantry in a semicircle facing forward, and then bending backwards.

"So I'm staying where I am, and will most likely enter the fighting at a later time?" Qarthalo asked.

"Exactly. Ah, Hasdrubal." Hannibal turned around and saw him, then looked back at the infantry officer. "All understood, Qarthalo?"

Qarthalo nodded in acknowledgement, and Hannibal motioned for Hasdrubal to follow him as he rode back along the line, to make sure the unusual new formation met his satisfaction.

"All in order on your wing?" the general asked him as they passed the furthest contingent of Gauls.

"Mainly. A few Gauls are a head short. You know the routine."

Hannibal grimaced. "A head short because they are looking for Roman ones, or because you chewed theirs off?"

"Both. In other words, my wing is in perfect order."

"That's reassuring. You heard me explaining about the tightened Roman infantry line and the crescent?"

"Yes."

"Good. Listen. The advantage for you, especially, is that it gives you marginally more space on your wing. When we've lured the Romans in with our centre facing forward, they'll push after. Wait." Hannibal interrupted himself as they rode by a noticeable forward bulge in the crescent, and he barked at an Iberian officer to get his men in line.

"So, the most important point," the general went on as the curve was even again and they continued along the line, "is that the Roman centre will be so condensed that we're going to draw up our Libyan trap all along its flank. *All* the way."

Hasdrubal narrowed his eyes. He could see what Hannibal was getting at, but by all the gods, he had never heard of anything like that before. "Catching a rat in a sack?"

He was rewarded with the rare spectacle of Hannibal blinking in confusion. "Rat? Sack?"

"Turn the sack inside out, put it over the rat, and turn it back right side out, so you won't get bitten."

Hannibal gave a bitter laugh. "Excellent. Though this rat will still bite."

Hasdrubal scratched his beard. "So if the flank attack is achieved completely by the Libyans..." He let his voice trail off.

"Yes."

"I'll be free for other... things."

"Yes."

"Like... pulling the string on the sack."

"Yes."

"That's insane." Hasdrubal brought his horse to a halt, but couldn't quite keep a glint out of his eye.

Hannibal grinned wolfishly. "I can see you're with me."

"I'm not sure that's a good thing. A rear attack?"

"Yes."

Hasdrubal had served with the Barcid army since the days of the general's father, when Hannibal had still been in his teens; thus, he had heard his share of wild ideas from him. At some of them, he still felt a slight urge to try and box some sense into the boy, even though the boy in question had long proven that his sense was excellent, and that even his wilder ploys usually worked.

"Complete encirclement?" Hasdrubal felt compelled to say. "Against seventy-thousand?"

Hannibal waved a hand dismissively. "I'm sure that some smart man has written a highly erudite treatment saying you must never encircle on both wings with a smaller army. He can keep it."

"Still sounds pretty erudite to me."

The younger man grabbed his shoulder, all banter aside. "Hasdrubal, listen. It's a *possibility*. I know it sounds staggering, but I say it's possible. I want you to use your judgment, nothing else. If you're needed on the flank after you've chased off your opponent, nothing changes. If you find that you're *not* needed... attack the Roman rear."

"With the utmost respect, general," Hasdrubal said in a low voice, a predatory grin creeping across his face, "your father'd have boxed you around the ears for this."

The corner of Hannibal's mouth curled into a grin to match Hasdrubal's. "Without a doubt. He never took it well when I saw something he didn't. Get back to your wing, and pray I'll never call you *Hasdrubal the Ratter* in public."

"What, then, is the difference?" the voice of Aemilius Paullus drifted over. "Opposite, you see mercenaries of a dozen different lands, brought together for one thing only: the prospect of pay. Now look at yourselves! The last hope of the fatherland, thousands of men with the same objective, all with the same goal: To preserve your families and the honour of Rome! To protect them from a barbarian horde that will murder your fathers, ravage your wives, enslave your children or sacrifice them to their cruel gods, burn your houses and pillage your temples, and erase the very memory of Rome from the face of the earth!"

A roar rang up from the assembled citizen cavalry, and Cornelius Lentulus felt his heart swell with fury.

"Sempronius probably told his men the same thing at the Trebia," Claudius Centho murmured under his breath.

Lentulus looked at him in irritation. "What sort of talk is that? Maybe he did. But the important thing is that, with the same courage on our side but a lack of possible traps on the enemy's, it's plain who will win this time."

"They're so many," Centho replied, his voice barely a whisper.

Lentulus followed the younger tribune's gaze. They couldn't see much of the enemy heavy cavalry that stood opposite them, and this was probably for the better; everyone on the right Roman wing knew how horribly outnumbered they were. If the numbers were true, there were more than two Spanish and Celtic horsemen for every Roman on this side of the field. At the very

thought, Lentulus' stomach did a slow, queasy roll.

"All we have to do is hold out," Lentulus said between his teeth. "This battle can't possibly last long. You'll see. Our superiority in infantry is so overwhelming – just imagine what eight legions must look like to them! It's a miracle they aren't running already. The Celts opposite us will be the first to run. You'll see."

"I'd feel better with some of the infantry here with us, to even the odds," Centho confessed.

"Infantry on the wings?" Lentulus asked, incredulous. "You're starting to sound like Publius Scipio. He's full of these things. Breaking up traditional orders. You heard him, back there."

"Dented centres, yes," Centho said. "I wonder if that means anything."

I'm not worried about dents in centres, Lentulus thought; *I'm starting to get more worried about foxes on riverbanks.* "I couldn't even begin to think how that would affect a battle," he replied. "Infantry on the wings, mixing allied and Roman contingents, breaking up a battle line. These things would just result in confusion among the soldiers." The thought alone was dizzying. "Honour and tradition, and the gods, will see Rome through once again, Marcus Claudius."

Lentulus took off his helmet, blinking back sweat as he stared into the sun, now hot and bright in his face. He wiped his forehead with the back of his hand, and put the helmet back on, his eyes on Aemilius Paullus, who now rode to take his position at the front lines of the right wing.

The sun had reached its zenith.

Hannibal was riding back along the line, now more and more crescent-shaped, shouting at officers or groups of stragglers to move into formation. Mago had done a remarkable job of putting the new formation into action; from what he could tell from where he stood, there was little left to be desired.

He had barely noticed how hot it had become until Bostar, one of his bodyguards, handed him a water flask. Hannibal gulped down a few swallows and gave it back, then, leaving Mago in his position in the centre, rode towards the skirmishers' line to see if all was ready, his guard falling into position close behind. Celtic, Gaetulan and Moorish spearmen, interspersed with the famed Balearic slingers, greeted him with loud war cries as he reached the foremost line.

Hannibal found Gisgo near the centre and surveyed the line, stretching almost half a mile in either direction.

"All is in formation, general," Gisgo reported as he reined in his horse next to him. Hannibal looked across the field. From here, the Roman lines looked much more formidable than they had hours ago, while he and Maharbal had watched them deploying.

Gisgo had followed the general's glance. "That's certainly a lot," he said with a nervous laugh, trying and failing to mask his fear.

Hannibal looked at the veritable forest of spears jutting up from the other side of the field, then back at Gisgo. "Yes, but you know – there is something rather amazing about them that has escaped your notice."

Gisgo blinked in confusion. "What do you mean?"

Hannibal touched his shoulder and pointed. "That, in all that number, there isn't a single man over there named Gisgo."

Gisgo's face reddened as the men around them, including Hannibal's guard, broke out in laughter. It was nervous laughter in some cases, born of mounting anxiety, but eventually, even Gisgo joined in. Hannibal caught his eye, and nodded at him as he clapped his shoulder. "You remember what I told you all this morning? I meant that." Gisgo put up a face of determination, mixed with some pride, and nodded.

Hannibal turned back, leaving Gisgo in charge, and made to return to his infantry line when a rider approached down the line from the right.

"General," the messenger panted. "Maharbal sends me. He says everyone

is in position."

Hannibal nodded. He sent the man back to Maharbal and turned his horse again. For just an instant, he wanted to ride up to the hill and take just one look at the battle lines, but he knew there was no time now for delay. Maharbal would have warned him if anything was amiss, or anything had changed on the Roman side. Hasdrubal knew exactly what was at stake, and would use his best judgment.

Hannibal found himself wishing, more than ever, that he could be in several places at once, but had to concede that Hasdrubal and Maharbal were the closest he would get to that wish.

This was the moment just before the start of battle that he had come to hate, and to accept – the feeling that there was still something left to do, to fix, to make even more impeccable, even though he was sure he and everyone around him had done their utmost. There would be no prize for the army that had deployed most beautifully.

The sun was wandering past its highest peak already, the heat would only become worse, and there was the danger of men dropping from exhaustion before the first spear had been cast. Unlike him, some of them had been standing in the same spot for hours, without anything to do but await a day of bloodshed.

The first stage was done. The pieces were set.

The *cornicen* beside Varro sounded three long, clear horn blasts. Immediately, the consul saw the line of *velites* ahead advancing, just as the signal was picked up by Carthaginian trumpeters across the field. Varro was at the head of the allied cavalry on the left flank, shielding his eyes against the sun with his hand. Turning to his right, his heart leaped at the sight of the legions, now in perfect formation, sun glinting on over seventy thousand helmets, over seventy thousand brightly painted shields. The pride of Rome, the largest army that had ever stood on Italian soil, was his to command. For generations to come, people would say that Gaius Terentius Varro had led Rome's legions into the Battle of Cannae. What a ring that had to it.

Ahead, the cries, roars and insults of the skirmishers were heard, picked up by the lines watching behind them and cheering them on. Both sides were armed with light spears that they now threw at the enemy; the Carthaginians had their slingers, with Paullus on the right wing stood a contingent of Cretan archers. The whir of sling-bullets filled the air, most of them aimed at the *velites* but some finding their way to the main Roman line. The riders at Varro's sides, Lucanian, Campanian, Samnite, and Etruscan, raised their shields, and most of the bullets fell harmless among his cavalry, or clattered off shields.

The skirmishers on both sides retreated a few steps, hurling insults rather than spears and bullets, then advanced afresh and renewed the attack. On the far side of the field, Varro saw the dark hail of arrows falling on the Carthaginian heavy cavalry. He could not see the effect, or even hear much apart from the general war cries and screams of the wounded, but he prayed that most of them had reached their mark – causing the first casualties and confusion in the ranks of the enemy horse.

Retreat again, more insults, more shouts of encouragement from the main lines. Over a hundred thousand men, most of them mere spectators at this stage, roaring out their fear and turning it into courage. Another salvo of spears and bullets and arrows. Behind Varro, some commotion as a horse buckled, hit in the forehead by a bullet. Retreat, cries, advance, and again retreat, longer pauses before the next advance, the insults getting shorter and more to the point as the skirmishers on both sides were becoming exhausted. The first few advances within striking distance, the first clashes man to man, with swords and daggers, retreat again, another breathless pause, another advance.

Finally, after several repeats of the same routine, a horn signal from the other side. The lines broke contact, many figures remaining wounded or dead upon the ground.

Varro signalled to the *cornicen*, and the man sounded the retreat for the *velites*. They hurled a last salvo of *pila* against the enemy, and under the cover of the commotion they caused, drew back. The centuries opened gaps for them to pass through – more seamlessly towards the flanks and the back of the lines, where the more experienced troops stood – and the *velites* trickled through to the back of the lines. The centuries closed ranks again, presenting their massive front to the enemy. Even before Varro could give the signal for the cavalry to attack, a cry went up opposite him, as the enemy's Numidians attacked.

Varro raised his sword and cried something that nobody would hear amid the roar answering the enemy's; he looked around and saw swords drawn among the tribunes, heavy spears hefted by the allies. The attack was sounded, barely audible above the din, as all around him, over three thousand horses fell into a trot.

The dust cloud beaten up by the Numidians reached them before the first spears did. Varro had heard tales about these riders, but some of his staff had already fought them. True enough, they fought more like skirmishers than cavalry, riding bareback on their stunted little ponies, which were incredibly fast and agile. Spears slammed into shields and clattered to the ground, but some found horses and men. One of Varro's bodyguard went down as his horse did, the man screaming as the animal rolled over him. The gods curse this dust. The two foremost lines around him returned the attack, casting their spears, but cast blind; when the dust shifted, Varro saw the Numidians already retreating, gathering, preparing their next assault. Curse the dust, and curse the Numidians.

"Forward!" the consul shouted over the snorting of horses, the clamour of the men. "They're scared of us! Form up! Close formation!"

His line reformed, and fell into another trot as the Numidians, too, advanced again.

Five hundred feet of space left between the Roman and Punic infantry lines.

It was a frightening spectacle and would always remain so. No matter how many times before they had beaten Roman legions, the sight of ten thousands of legionaries advancing was enough to make one's bowels knot.

Bomilkar thanked the gods that his did no more than knot. His nose told him that, somewhere in his vicinity, someone else's bowels had done the complete opposite. He couldn't fault the poor sod. Neither did his comrades. It hap-pened, and by silent agreement, everyone pretended that it didn't.

They stood still, waiting, letting the Romans approach. That alone was almost impossible to bear, but Bomilkar knew it had to do with the precarious half-moon formation. In march, that would be impossible to keep up, would open gaps that would invite breakthroughs, and disaster. He briefly closed his eyes as he fingered the small enamelled ram's head amulet he wore around his neck, which his eldest daughter had given him before he had left Iberia. Neither he, nor his wife, or daughters could have known that the march would take him a thousand miles away, across mountains and rivers and swamps, and that he would not see them for three years. He kissed the amulet, for luck,

and tucked it back into his linen cuirass.

Four hundred feet. Time seemed to go so slowly. He could see them marching, and yet they didn't seem to get any closer. *Come here already, you bastards. Let's get this over with so we can go home.*

Not *pilum* range by far. Across the field, the Romans were raising war-cries and clashing their weapons to shields. Around Bomilkar, the cries were taken up. Most of the men directly around were Celts; he couldn't be sure if it was actual words they roared, or just fear made audible. How could the men

around him sound so fearful, and the ones across the field so ferocious?

Maybe it sounded the other way round from where they marched.

Three hundred feet. Some of the Celts threw the first spears, which fell short by a long way. Officers yelled at them for wasting weapons. Hannibal, too, was shouting, turning right and left and right again, reminding the men of their past victories he had led them to, sitting up straight in the saddle. The sight of the general presenting such a clear target filled Bomilkar with familiar dread, but he told himself that it was still safe. Still well out of *pilum* range.

Two hundred feet. Still so incredibly far away. The moment seemed to stretch endlessly. Bomilkar remembered the agony of waiting in ambush at the battle of Lake Trasimene, the previous summer, for hours, until they finally heard the Roman army below them, invisible in the mist as they walked into the waiting trap, completely unawares, lambs to the slaughter. Now, it seemed like the complete opposite. The Romans were still marching, they were still waiting, but this time, the Romans saw them.

A hundred feet. They were close enough now to make out faces, contorted with rage and fear and hatred. Bomilkar did not need to look around himself to know that the men next to him wore the same expressions, men who had made jokes at his expense when they saw him scouring the camp at dawn, who had shared their porridge and oil with him, and who had taught him to say "your mother fucks goats" in Ligurian, in exchange for Libyan. He drew closer to Hannibal's horse, raising his shield.

Orders from the chieftains and the officers to ready spears. A voice raised over the others opposite. Bomilkar caught one Latin word. *Pila*.

A shudder went through the Punic line as the first spears rang among them. Most fell short; some struck into shields and unprotected calves and feet. Bomilkar held his shield at arm's length; that way, if a *pilum* struck

through it, it wouldn't reach him. A few feet to his right, one of the Celts fell; he had crouched close behind his shield, instinctively, to protect himself, and the *pilum* had struck right through shield and body. Among the Roman line, some spears had also hit. The advance slowed down momentarily. The first blood had been drawn, and every instinct refused to get even closer, and repeat the routine. More spears were thrown, and then a second volley of *pila* fell. Two rows in front of Bomilkar, a Celt went down, screaming as he tried to draw out the spear transfixing his foot to the ground.

Fifty feet. The Roman line suddenly seemed so close, as if they had flown the last stretch. Bomilkar's stomach twisted. He wondered if this ever stopped, after a hundred battles. With luck, he would never know. He had heard Hannibal say that this battle would likely end the war.

One way or the other.

He could see the sun glinting on leaden spearheads as the fourth and fifth lines opposite raised their *pila*, and threw.

Beside him, a few men trying to shrink back, others pushing behind, orders being shouted. Bomilkar felt a hiss of cool air as a *pilum* shot across his head, then orders shouted behind him turned into a scream as it hit someone at his back. A quick glance; a Punic junior officer. None of his own men. Not Hannibal.

Twenty feet, fifteen, ten. A group of Celts roaring and charging, no officer calling them back. More Celts and some Iberians pushing after, into the gap. A short hesitation in the ranks opposite of them. A flash of fear across some of the faces, on others, determination.

Bomilkar shot a silent prayer to Shadrapha and Tanit, and added one to Melqart for good measure. He kept his eyes firmly on the Roman line from behind his shield all the while, scanning for missiles that might come his way.

Then the distance was gone as if it had never been, swallowed by marching feet. The two lines clashed amid a deafening noise, as men stabbed from behind shields, pushed, shuffled back, advanced again, soldiers falling and shouting and yelling and screaming, horses snorting in fear. The noise drowned out the occasional sound of steel piercing meat, making everything seem oddly detached, like someone else's experience. *Pila*, shields, swords, faces, dust. And Hannibal at his left, in the midst of it all, protected by his shield, and his prayers.

The world was red. It had no business being red.

"Lucius Aemilius! Can you hear me? *Aemilius!*"

A voice, close to his ear, and further away, the sounds of battle.

Battle. He couldn't sleep here. By the gods, was it day already?

Aemilius Paullus blinked a few times, and the world reverted to its usual colours. The battle sounds remained. The face of young Cornelius Lentulus was close to his, almost blocking out an incredibly blue sky.

"Aemilius!" Lentulus said again, relief mixing into the alarm in his features.

Through a haze in his mind that refused to recede, Paullus fought to make sense of his surroundings. He was shielded by his bodyguard, a hundred feet towards the back of his cavalry force. The cries, grunts and screams of men and

horses made it clear immediately that the fighting in the front lines was fierce.

As he tried to get to his feet, throbbing pain in his temple hit him without warning. Lentulus motioned for Aurelius Cotta, another tribune, to support him, and he managed to stand. When the consul touched a hand to his forehead, it came away bloody. He noticed that Cotta was holding his helmet. "What happened?" he asked.

"A sling-bullet. Half deflected by your helmet. Can you stand?"

"My horse," the consul demanded.

Furius, his quaestor, led up the consul's horse, and Cotta helped him to mount. Paullus put his helmet back on his head, secured the strap under his chin. His head did not stop throbbing, and the helmet made it worse. "The battle?"

He saw the tribunes exchanging glances, and those, together with what he was hearing, were enough for him. He had always known that his would be the hardest lot on the field today, matched against Hannibal's heavy cavalry, but his men were not yet fleeing, and by Castor and Pollux, if he could prevent it, he would.

"Where's the Carthaginian?" he slurred, seeing that a dispatch rider was standing next to Furius. "Does anyone know? Is it him we're facing?"

"They say he's in the centre with his Celtic and Spanish troops," the rider replied.

Paullus nodded. So Hannibal, too, had chosen to position himself at the weakest spot of his army. He felt a grudging respect for the man.

"Guards!" he cried, briefly catching himself as a spell of vertigo came and passed. "To me!" At once, his bodyguard took their positions around him as he pressed on to the front ranks of the battle, and shouts and cheers rang up as the men saw that their consul was there, still with them, still leading them. The fighting in the front line had been bitter; dead and dying men and thrashing horses littered the ground, and the space was so tight that many combatants had dismounted or dragged their foes to the ground. The Carthaginian line – if it could be called Carthaginian; most of what Paullus saw looked Celtic – was momentarily beaten back by the renewed vigour of his men.

The consul cast a brief look to his left, but even from horseback, it was impossible to tell how the battle was going. The infantry lines had met; beyond the middle of the formation, everything was lost in clouds of dust. His cavalry were being beaten severely, but they still succeeded in presenting a solid front to the enemy. They hadn't broken. He told himself that, over and over; if he could only hold out a little longer, then victory would be theirs.

Maharbal hissed a curse as he watched the tightly knotted masses of Gallic, Spanish, African, and Roman cavalry on the left wing, tangled into each other beyond recognition. His horse snorted and pranced, sensing his own tension. There was nothing more he could discern from where he stood. The Numidian cavalry on the right was doing what it did best – neutralising the Roman auxiliary horse and keeping them occupied, slowly grinding away at them without losing many of its own.

He had had one messenger from Hannibal a good while ago; since then, nothing.

Half an hour into the battle, an attack had come on the Punic camp, launched from that of Paullus; Maharbal, trusting in the eight-thousand garrison that Hannibal had left there, sent messengers to Hannibal, but didn't intervene.

On the left flank, the cavalry battle was taking too long. Too bloody long. Cries, shouts and shrieks from the centre had joined those from the flanks half an hour ago, when the centres had clashed; at first, Hannibal's men had held out and stood their ground, then the mass had pushed them back. Immediately, Hannibal had withdrawn, reforming during a short breathing space, then advancing once more, the Romans pushing after. Already, the crescent had flattened considerably. Maharbal had watched in amazement as the Roman centre did exactly what Hannibal had predicted they would. The battering ram, encountering no door to push against, was spending itself uselessly. The men on the outsides were pressing inward, the Roman infantry mass becoming denser and the frontage shorter, its shape no longer an ordered rectangle but more and more turning into a ragged blob.

But it was still a ragged blob of ten thousands of fresh, highly motivated fighters.

The sun had wandered, now standing directly at the Punic army's back and dropping. Two hours past noon. About six, seven hours of daylight left. Too bloody long.

Maharbal rode down, telling his dispatch riders and horn-blowers to accompany him. He would not be able to get through to Hannibal in person, but maybe he might glean some bit of information about the battle in the centre, to determine how long it might hold.

He found Monomachos conversing with his second-in-command on the right flank as he approached.

"Maharbal!" Monomachos greeted him. His face looked flushed, although his troops had not seen any action; the columns of Libyans still stood behind

and at some distance to the rest of the centre. Maharbal knew only too well where Monomachos' restlessness was coming from – for him, waiting idly was even less bearable than it was to Maharbal. "Does that mean we attack?"

"What – no!" Maharbal quickly looked between Monomachos and the far-away front to his left. "Have you had any messengers?"

"The last one was an hour ago." Monomachos spat. "Damn it, he can't want us to stand around here for hours when we could be more useful elsewhere!"

"He can, and he does," Maharbal replied with an edge to his voice. In this kind of mood, Monomachos could be difficult to deal with. Maharbal was glad he had chosen to ride to Monomachos, not Qarthalo; the latter would find it easier to trust in Hannibal's orders and not try anything rash. "Have you been able to learn anything?"

Monomachos gestured. "He's being driven back," he said. "His line will break."

"Is that your observation or Hannibal's or Mago's actual words?"

"I told you, I haven't had any messages. But that's plain enough. Half an hour, maybe. Fuck, he could have ended up on the end of a *pilum* for all we know!"

"He couldn't," Maharbal said sharply, his hand twitching as he resisted the urge to make the sign against evil to ward off bad luck, telling himself it was absurd even to consider it. "You think they'd still be fighting like that if he had?"

"He said to bring in the Libyans as reinforcements if things go bad. Things are going bad. Maybe he's in no position to give the order."

"He also said to act on his signal, or on mine. He hasn't given it, and neither am I. Stay in your position. *That's* an order."

Monomachos' nostrils flared, but he said nothing. His horse stamped, and he curbed it with a sharp tug on the reins.

"If Hannibal really is in no position to give the order," Maharbal went on, "You will get it from me the instant the line breaks, not a moment sooner."

"That'll be too late!" Monomachos shouted in frustration.

"I'm carrying out his orders, and you're going to do the same." Maharbal forced his voice to carry all the calm determination he could, told himself what he was dealing with wasn't blatant insubordination, but a great deal of helplessness. Monomachos had also been a close friend of Hannibal's for years. "Tanit Face of Baal, have some faith."

Monomachos again restrained his restlessly prancing horse. "Faith," he repeated.

"Yes, faith." Maharbal half-turned his own horse, and called to his messengers. "It's all going according to plan. We knew today wouldn't be easy. Stay where you are."

He held Monomachos' eyes for long enough to be sure there wouldn't be any unsanctioned swipes, then he gave him another affirmative nod and rode on, to the Numidian cavalry fight, to see how things stood on the right wing.

What information had he gained? Bloody nothing. Apart from the rather unsavoury mental image of Hannibal on the end of a spear.

Bomilkar grunted with the impact of something hitting his shield. The tip of the *pilum* nicked his right shoulder before the thickened portion of its shaft stopped its progress through wood and leather. Cursing, Bomilkar fell back, Bostar moving past him to take his place at Hannibal's right while Bomilkar dealt with the situation. He tugged at the *pilum*, but the leaden shaft had twisted on impact, and he couldn't draw it out no matter how he tried. With another, much more flowery curse, he cast away the shield and swung off his horse, ducking as he dragged a discarded shield from under its dead Celtic owner and picked it up. It, too, had two *pila* protruding from it. Unluckily for the Celt, they had been the lighter, thinner ones, and they had gone straight through shield and man. Luckily for Bomilkar, he was able to

draw both out. It was a large, oval infantry shield, too large to be comfortably carried on horseback, but the time to be picky was long past. At least it could be wielded with the right hand – Celtic shields were usually very useful in that respect, as Bomilkar had long found out.

It was a pause in the fighting. Hannibal had drawn back the line once more, the Romans doing the same, making use of the short breathing space it brought them. Finding shields to replace useless ones would be much easier for the Romans – it was them who were advancing across the bodies of the dead and dying left in the middle.

Field medics, specialist soldiers armoured like the rest of the men, were moving around and binding up wounds in a hurry, concentrating on those who could reasonably be helped. Most of the men were bleeding from cuts to arms and legs, some tottered with bleeding faces.

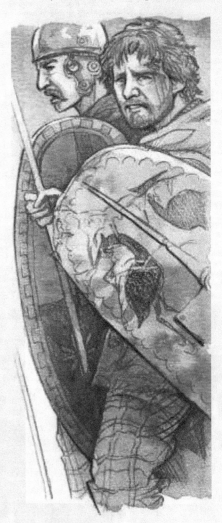

The Baleareans, now positioned close to the fighting front, moved in at every pause and kept up showers of bullets at the enemy. Most of them were down to using stones from the ground, or even hardened chunks of loam.

A few spears flew from both sides; the *pilum* that had cost Bomilkar his shield had been one of few lucky hits through the first rank. Sweat was running from under his helmet. The padding inside it had long given up its usefulness in soaking it up, now acting like a very wet sponge instead, dousing him with trickles of his own sweat whenever he moved.

The men all around were just as ex-haust-ed. Bomilkar saw in their faces that bleary, wild look of battle pau-ses, in which the mind went into that blank state between utmost aggression and utmost fear. A few wounded were dragged back through the ranks, a few fresh fighters replacing them, the aggression and fear in their faces yet undimmed by the blankness that always came after the first blood.

Hannibal was talking to a few of the Celtic chieftains. Like everyone around him, the general was covered with yellow dust and spattered with blood, but Bomilkar knew – or prayed – that most of it wasn't his. The guard captain didn't understand what was being said, but there were words that Hannibal had been using over and over for the last two hours. Bomilkar remembered overhearing Hannibal – two or three nights ago; or possibly a hundred – repeating Celtic words and phrases to himself in his tent after talking to one of his translators.

Urging their horses on, they passed the next contingent of Iberians; Hannibal spoke to a few of the men, to one or two of the junior officers, words of encouragement and perseverance. Himilko, one of his guards, passed Bomilkar a water skin. He drank, and then handed it on to Hannibal.

With Hannibal stood a few dispatch riders; there weren't many of them now. Bomilkar looked at the battle line. It seemed incredibly long. It took him a while to realise that the crescent was gone; flattened out on both sides. Was that good or bad? Was it too early? What was too early anyway? He had no idea. He wasn't quite sure what the purpose of the crescent had been in the first place; he had listened as Hannibal explained it to his officers, but it was none of his business. His business was simple. Keep Hannibal alive.

A cry rang up from the Roman soldiers on the other side of the field, heralding the end of the fighting break. Hannibal thrust the water skin back at Himilko; the guard hastened to stopper it again and fasten it to his saddle. As Bomilkar saw the Roman ranks advancing, he suddenly registered, with a sick, leaden feeling in his insides, that they were still *hastati*. The Celts and Iberians around them were almost through all their reserves from the back of the line; and the Romans opposite were still fighting with their first ranks. No, they had to be *principes*.

Tanit Face of Baal, let them be principes. *I just didn't look properly, that's all.*

P aullus saw it happen, but couldn't believe how it *could* have happened. He had held the line, more and more desperately, as more warriors in the confined space had dismounted to fight on foot. The throbbing in his temple was ebbing on and off; at one point, overcome with dizziness from the heat and from his wound, he had slipped off his horse, causing his bodyguard and, to his dismay, more and more of the riders around him to dismount as well. He had shouted at them to get back on their horses. A few had heard. Most had not. Someone had thought to relay his command, but there was not enough order, and too much noise, in his ranks to spread it. The Celts and Iberians, with their long slashing swords, were hacking at shoulders and heads and necks, wreaking havoc on any man on foot. In the small spaces where there was room to swing a sword, battle turned into butchery. And little by little, those spaces were growing.

He was back on his horse now, his bodyguard much reduced, blocking sword slashes and returning them. His ears were ringing with the sound of metal on metal and wood and flesh, the screams of the dead and dying. It was difficult to breathe in the sweltering heat, the clogging dust. The muscles in his arms were burning. Still he held the line. Or did he? His men weren't breaking. He clung to this thought as to a prayer. They weren't breaking. He was doing his duty. He was holding the line.

A cry went up ahead and, incredibly, to the left, where they should have been protected by the right infantry flank. For a moment of senseless dismay, Paullus thought that, somehow, by whatever treachery, the battle in the centre was lost, the army routed; then he saw it was still there, but carried away in the relentless fighting. But the enemy cavalry was no longer pinned as spaces opened that had not been there before. Suddenly, they broke over them, from the flank, and through the gaps in the front.

The few of the Roman riders that were still mounted shrank back in shock, and the shock rippled through what remained of his men, like a drop of water sending out longer and longer circles across the surface. Some at the end of the lines turned their horses and started to run.

The men around him still weren't breaking. As a renewed attack from the Iberians and Gauls hit them, most of them were simply cut down where they stood.

With a mournful sound cutting strangely through the screams and shouts, his horse stumbled and went down; he hadn't even noticed that a spear had buried itself deep in its chest. Paullus struggled to get up, leaning upon something that turned out to be the body of Cotta. The tribune's eyes were open, and he was staring sightlessly up at the sky. It was still blue. It almost surprised him.

Cornelius Lentulus appeared at his side, with a spare mount – Cotta's? His mouth was moving, but Paullus couldn't hear.

The tribune's mouth moved again.

"What?"

His own voice broke the spell. That of Lentulus drifted into his ears. "Lucius Aemilius! The right wing is lost!"

Paullus nodded numbly. It took him three attempts to mount the horse. Of his bodyguard, only one man was left. Claudius Centho, the only remaining tribune besides Lentulus, stayed next to the consul, to keep him on his horse.

"The centre," Paullus slurred. "Into the centre." The Carthaginian was there. If he could only get through to the centre, renew the attack, and take out Hannibal, the Carthaginian's army would still break.

Lentulus looked at him, nodded mutely. They gathered as many men as they could, and made for the standard of the Twelfth, barely visible in the dust ahead.

Hasdrubal was reforming his troops amid the carnage, shouting orders when Maharbal met up with him. To Maharbal, the place beside the riverbank looked surreal. When he had last seen it, from a distance, it had been a coiling mass of horses and men; now, they stood on a field of waste strewn with bodies. A few riderless horses with Roman tack were stepping between them, jumping at noises and sudden movements. Scattered groups of enemies were disappearing in the distance; the rest lay dead and dying on the field. Maharbal was amazed at the way Hasdrubal had managed to keep his men in hand; one group of Celts had given chase, but apart from them, there was no pursuit. The infantry line seemed incredibly far away.

"How are things on the right wing?" Hasdrubal asked without preamble. The service corps officer appeared unscathed.

"Undecided," Maharbal said. "Numidian. I haven't been able to talk to Hanno, but to that junior officer of his... Gulussa. Few losses, he says, but the Roman cavalry is still on the field. Our camp is being attacked."

Hasdrubal grimaced. "How bad?"

"Holding out." Maharbal exhaled sharply. "The centre is the problem."

"How far's that?" Hasdrubal asked.

"Retreating. Still. Look at the space that gave you. It's caving in. I don't think he can keep this up much longer."

"Ah." Hasdrubal stared into nothingness; Maharbal could see his thoughts racing as their horses stamped uneasily, foam dripping from their muzzles.

"Don't expose the flank," Maharbal warned.

"Yes, I will. The flank is in no danger – the crescent formation has seen to that. And I've had a rider from him. He says he can hold out for another hour, possibly more."

"He can *what*?" Maharbal repeated, incredulous. "That's insane, Hasdrubal. There is no bloody way he can hold out that long. It's bordering on a miracle he's even made it this far. We're pushing our luck with every moment – damn it, I've seen it! Attack the Roman flank. That'll mess up his plan, but will prevent a disaster."

"*You* have seen it, but *he* says he can hold the centre. Whom do I believe? *Your* eyes, or *his* gut? Your decision. But be quick about it."

The two of them stared at each other. Maharbal's jaws were working. He realised that this, if nothing else, was the moment that might secure a victory beyond any of their wildest dreams, or bring about utter defeat. Hannibal didn't have the complete picture, but did he need that to know how close the centre was to breaking? And hadn't he predicted that everything would unfold in exactly this way?

Maharbal spat a curse.

"His gut, damn it," he whispered. "Because if you believe my eyes, and they prove wrong, he'd probably gouge them out. And if you believe his gut, and that proves wrong, we're all dead anyway."

"Now don't you get too optimistic." Hasdrubal wheeled his horse around. "Have some trust in him."

"I have all the trust in the world in Hannibal; it's the Celts I'm worried about!"

"Ah, the Celts are better than their reputation. Most of them." Hasdrubal grimaced. "How many do you need to relieve the camp?"

Maharbal chewed on his lower lip. "Give me seven hundred. How many have you lost?"

"I can spare eight hundred. Take care of that camp. I'm taking care of the allied horse. Now we'll see what that crescent was worth!" He quickly signalled for two squadron officers, one Celtic, one Iberian, to draw off their units and go with Maharbal. Then he sounded the rally, and had his troops fall into a trot.

Maharbal stood by the riverbank, watching the heavy cavalry sweeping down the river to the northeast, around the Roman rear in a wide circle, with the ghastly feeling that he had made a horrible mistake.

Another onslaught, ringing shields, stabbing swords, flying *pila*. How could they still have *pila*? Why weren't they running out of them?

Hannibal brought up his shield to defend against one of the thrown spears; it rang close to his ear and clattered off. It was becoming harder and harder to find shields that were usable; Hannibal had somehow found himself with an absurdly ornamental round bronze shield that looked as if one of his Celts might have looted it from an Etruscan grave. It was too heavy by any means to be wielded easily (and he couldn't shake the thought that this was what had killed its previous bearer), but it had the distinct advantage that a *pilum* couldn't stick in it.

A handful of legionaries broke through the ranks of Celts in front of him. Hannibal could see the look in their eyes – the face of victory. His bodyguard moved in to stop them; Bostar fell, with spear in his face, and Bomilkar hacked down one of the attackers with his curved *falcata*. The muscles in Hannibal's left arm protested as he deflected a sword-thrust, and then struck between helmet and shield in front of him. As the Roman went down, his gurgle sounding almost the same as Bostar's, two more took his place. A Spanish swordsman, formerly white tunic so spattered with blood as to be almost indistinguishable from the purple borders, struck at one of the attackers before he reeled back from a shield thrust. Hannibal's horse suddenly slumped to the side with a

strangled sound in its throat. He barely managed to scramble off the animal's back as it rolled over, kicking feebly, a *pilum* through its neck. Himilko caught Hannibal's arm to steady him, and offered him his horse. Hannibal nodded wordlessly as he mounted, and immediately, his bodyguard pushed him back. There was not even time to put the animal out of its misery.

All these things registered, but triggered nothing. He was left with little that wasn't a mechanical action.

The group of *hastati* that had broken into his ranks quickly paid for their brashness. They wounded or killed a handful of his men, before a group of Celtic warriors moved in and stabbed and slashed at their exposed sides and backs. One of them doubled back, defending himself with his large shield until he found his way back into his own rank; the others were cut down.

It had been the fourth of these breakthroughs Hannibal had witnessed in front of him; they were getting more numerous, or so it felt to him. With sudden clarity, he realised his line was only a few setbacks away from being routed. A horrible leaden feeling spread across his insides. The gods help him, he had been so sure that he could make this work.

"Back! Back! Retreat!"

Hannibal's voice was nearly gone, his throat dry and raw from shouting orders and breathing in dust in the sweltering heat, but the horn-blower at his left heard him – or maybe he'd only seen his lips moving – and sounded the signal. For the eighth or ninth time, the lines in front of him broke apart, and as they had the previous times, the numbers of Celts and legionaries that remained lying in the middle were similar. His soldiers were still holding their own against the Romans.

One of the men closest to him, pushing with his shield to break away from his opponent, reeled back and crashed into Hannibal's horse. The animal threw its head, and he had difficulty getting it back under control. He patted the horse's neck to calm it. Its coat was slick with sweat. Hannibal coughed

and spat out something yellow.

The general caught Bomilkar's inquiring face and just nodded to signal he was unhurt, then turned around again to talk to one of the Iberian chieftains, to send more Baleareans to join the second and third ranks. He had long thrown in the last fresh reserves, and was down to bringing in the lightly wounded and the skirmishers. A few exhausted words with a Celt, dragging up a dizzy Iberian who was otherwise unhurt, more words of encouragement. The men needed to see him, needed to draw courage from the fact that he was there with them, still confident, still undaunted. They needed to see that

they had not lost yet.

Hannibal turned to look around. He wasn't even sure what direction he was facing anymore. The sun didn't seem to have moved at all for hours; the river wasn't where it should have been, either. Reason told him he must have turned with the sun, but as much as he tried to rotate his internal map to match what he was seeing, it wouldn't fit, and it irritated him. He didn't know where Hasdrubal was with the heavy cavalry, or the Libyans, or Hanno, or Maharbal, or even Mago. For a while now, no dispatch riders had made it through to him. The world had shrunk down to a hundred feet of frontage, of deafening noise, of Celts and Iberians behind and of legions in front, of cries and whirring bullets, of necks and shoulders and helmets and shields and victory-flushed faces between them, of dead and dying men.

Some thirty feet to his right and left, the men had drawn back; beyond that, they were still fighting, or already fighting once more.

The breaks in the fighting occurring along each little stretch of frontage were becoming longer. The sun was beating down relentlessly, and none of the men around him had any water left. The dust stinging in his eyes was maddening; at least, Hannibal thought as he rubbed at his right eye, *that* couldn't get any worse. The thought was vaguely gratifying, and the pain took his mind off his fears.

The Romans were showing signs of exhaustion, too, having to advance across the bodies of dead enemies and dead comrades, left behind by the retreat of the Punic centre. Still, it was them who always ended the breaks to advance afresh. Initially, Hannibal had tried to have his men attack first, for some psychological edge; by now, he had realised he couldn't keep it up. Letting the Romans come at them meant a few more moments between onslaughts, a few more moments to enable them to hold out longer, a few more moments for the cavalry.

Every moment counted now. And every moment seemed twice as long as the last.

"Aemilius!" The shock showed on proconsul Servilius Geminus' face at the sight of the consul. Paullus could see that he was on the verge of asking a question, but didn't voice it – afraid that what he might ask would turn out to be true.

Lentulus answered the unasked question. "The right wing is lost."

Servilius didn't speak, and neither did Paullus. He had faltered once or twice on their way here; his wound was bothering him, and the heat had become almost unbearable, but he was determined to hold on. Three dozen men had made it with them, among them Centho, Furius, the consul's quaestor, and Lentulus. Their path had been chaotic. For some reason they didn't fully understand, the battle lines were in disarray; Paullus put it down to the troops' inexperience. Order in the entire centre was mostly gone; most of the maniples were dissolved into ragged, intermingling structures in a constant forward push, centurions and optios fighting to get their units together as they pressed after a retreating enemy. The lack of order was hardly reassuring, but it would soon be over, and order was of little consequence when the battle was won. Servilius appeared unhurt. Bullets were flying here, too; the clanging of stones on metal was almost deafening, cutting any discussion short.

The proconsul had shouted to a tribune further back during a breathing space, to bring in fresh reinforcements from the back of the line. Exhausted, lightly wounded *hastati* withdrew, dragging more badly wounded comrades with them, to be replaced by fresh *principes*, each of the men with two *pila*. They threw them across the gap at the enemy line, then closed ranks to advance.

Servilius gestured ahead, to the Carthaginian battle line. "We're driving them back," the proconsul shouted over the din. "They've held out, remarkably for those savages, but we're forcing breakthroughs in their line. Not long now, and they'll be running, and the day will be ours."

"Any news from Varro?" shouted Centho.

Servilius shook his head.

But that was a good thing, Paullus thought. They would know if the left wing was lost as well. They had the stronger cavalry on the left wing, facing the weaker Punic cavalry. For a moment he vaguely wondered whether balancing the wings some more might have been a good idea after all.

The consul nodded. Centho was at his side, unobtrusively supporting him. Paullus blinked back the bright points of light dancing at the edge of his field of vision as he sat up erect in the saddle, drew his sword and shouted encouragement to the men. Paullus saw Lentulus moving close to Centho, shouting something into his ear. Over the din, Paullus could not hear what it was, but the tribunes' worried expressions made it easy enough to guess   to keep the consul out of the fighting.

Paullus shook his head emphatically, reeled, but gestured ahead. With an apologetic look at Lentulus, Centho advanced close to Paullus, protecting the consul with his own shield. Lentulus followed suit, taking his place at the consul's right.

A few ranks before them, the first legionaries clashed once more with the enemy. Paullus did not raise another cry; he contented himself with being present and visible, despite his wound. More bullets whirred through the air. One clanged noisily against Lentulus' shield, and another hit the helmet of Furius Bibaculus. Then the enemy line in front of them began to stagger back; Paullus saw frightened faces opposite as legionaries charged into their ranks. Everywhere around them, a cry went up as his men charged.

"**N**o. No, no, no, no, *fuck, no.*" Maharbal had led his relief force of eight hundred Iberian and Celtic cavalry across the river. Hannibal's camp garrison had held its own as well as it could against the attacking Romans; Maharbal's approach had dispersed the attack so that the camp had regained the upper hand.

From his high vantage point of the hills on the left bank, ready to ride back to his position, Maharbal now looked back at the battle. Only the back ranks of the Punic centre could be made out from here, but what he saw, half hidden in the dust and the distance, was a small trickle of men pouring out from the main infantry line.

Whatever it was, it was not supposed to happen.

Cursing under his breath all the while, he drew off his dispatch riders and horn-blowers, leaving the Iberian and Celtic officers in charge of the cavalry squadrons, and raced back down towards the river as fast as he could force his mount downhill. He almost missed the ford, earning himself an involuntary

douse as his horse suddenly missed its step and plunged into the Aufidus, before scrambling back to higher ground.

Make use of whatever unit is available, Hannibal had told him. Now he was looking at an army close to being routed, and the only force available to him were a handful of messengers... and two trumpeters.

He spat out a mouthful of water. "Ride to the flanks, and sound the signal for the flank attack!" he told the two men, as soon as they had forded the river. "*Go!*" he bellowed, when they didn't get their flustered horses under control fast enough.

They raced off, one straight north to the left wing, the other northeast to the right. Maharbal now saw what the outpouring had been, and his worst fears were confirmed. There were Celts, and Roman legionaries pursuing them. The centre had broken. Not all along the line, but at least in two places that he could see.

In the northeast he heard, or prayed he heard, the signal for the Libyans, just as, in front of him, he saw Celts being slaughtered.

Let it be in time... for fuck's sake, let it be in time.

Hannibal called the line to a retreat yet again, and yet again, he almost feared the legionaries would not let them. The enemy, too, was exhausted, more from waiting than from actual fighting; but it was still enough to make them break away, to give his men a short, much needed breathing space. The men around him were staggering; even some of those who were unhurt could barely stand on their feet. There did not seem to be many now who were unhurt. His bodyguard was down to three men – Bomilkar, Himilko, and the Iberian Abartiaigis. Apart from the general, only Bomilkar was still mounted.

Hannibal rode back one or two ranks to stop the retreat at the right time, to make sure nobody ran. Behind him, the ranks were only five men deep now, and two of those were made up of slingers. Panting, he drew the back of his

right hand across his face to wipe sweat from his eyes, and ended up smearing blood all over it.

"General. Let me look at that."

Blinking in irritation, Hannibal looked at the field medic that had appeared at his side, then down at himself. He was perplexed to see a deep sword wound in his right thigh, unable to remember how or when that had happened. It must have bled a lot, to judge by the dark clotted blood all down his saddle, but he hadn't even felt it, much less seen it amid all the blood that everyone around was coated with. He did feel it now, as if it had only winked into existence the moment he saw it. Like a signal his body had been waiting for, he suddenly felt everything else too, but couldn't even distinguish between aching muscles and actual cuts and bruises.

The medic bound up his leg to staunch the bleeding, but as he was about to turn to other injuries, Hannibal shook his head and pushed the man away. There was no time.

There were loud cries some twenty feet to his right. For a heartbeat, the world appeared to freeze as he saw legionaries charging into the ranks between a group of Celts and Iberians, not a scattered group as before, but what seemed to be an endless stream. His ranks were backing away, and then the first of his men turned to run.

Something happened to his perception then. His field of vision seemed to narrow down, his focus closing in, until all he could see, could even think about, was the breach.

"Close the ranks!" he shouted hoarsely, urging his horse forward, not looking back to see if his bodyguard was keeping up. "Stand and fight!" he wanted to add, but this time, barely any sound came out.

So be it, then. If words failed, actions would have to serve.

He rode between the breaking Iberians and Celts, bodily holding several of them back. The men around stared at him. Two kept running. The others rallied around him, to beat back the *principes* that had broken through their ranks.

Monomachos and Qarthalo. He needed the flank attack, *now*.

Wildly, Hannibal looked around for his horn-blowers. There should have been two in his immediate vicinity, but he couldn't see any of them. They must have been separated from him, or killed, when the ranks broke. There was only one dispatch rider near. Hannibal grabbed the man, and an Iberian officer who was likewise mounted.

"The flank attack!" he shouted at the dispatch rider. "Ride to Monomachos! Now!"

The man guessed rather than heard his words, after the second repeat, shook himself, and raced away, giving the groups of legionaries a wide berth.

It took longer to tell the Iberian officer what he was to do. The man's task was to keep his unit together, not to relay messages from a general whose voice was almost gone. At last, with the help of Abartiaigis, Hannibal was sure he had got it. As the officer finally galloped away to the left flank, Hannibal felt utterly drained.

No time for that, either.

His guard had been shielding him while he had been giving the orders; now, he urged his horse towards the attackers again, the mixed group of scattered Iberians and Celts plus a few slingers forming up around them. The legionaries' advance had been briefly slowed at the renewed resistance, but they soon resumed their charge, quite obviously realising what the high number of men in linen and bronze cuirasses meant. None of them had any of their *pila* anymore, but they now charged at them, swords in hand. Behind them, more were pouring through the breach. Hannibal and the group following him were back in the ranks now, close to the gaping hole. He prayed that his presence would keep his men around him from fleeing, but soon he realised, oddly detached, that none of his efforts was going to close the gap. He clung to this state of detachment, which kept the icy feeling of desolation at bay. A quick glance along the line to his left told him that more breaches were opening, as in more places, the Romans started to break through, his men unable to withstand the pressure. A sword grazed Hannibal's right arm as he stabbed at a man in front of him; behind him, Himilko dropped his weapon, cursing and gasping, cradling bloody fingers to his side. He did not retreat. There was nowhere to retreat now.

Still the flow continued. One of the enemies thrust at Hannibal with a long spear. He deflected the thrust, and saw Bomilkar cutting the man down, the guard's *falcata* slicing through the Roman's mail shirt.

Long spear. Mail shirt.

Triarii.

This one thought suddenly pierced Hannibal's blind, detached focus, like a brief flash of light. If there was a single *triarius* here, breaking through far ahead of his comrades from the last ranks of the Roman infantry, that could only mean one thing.

Complete disarray in the Roman centre.

By all the gods. So close. *So close.*

There was a roaring sound in Hannibal's ears as he desperately fought to keep the line together, keep his men from breaking, at least in spots, at least in this one spot, at least for a little while longer.

So close.

Suddenly, the onslaught lessened. The roaring did not stop.

Then the sounds registered. It was not a sound in his ears at all, but came from across the line. It wasn't the war-cries, the clanging of sword against shield, the triumphant yells, but cries and screams, broken apart by a few bellowed orders, and then, more screams of thousands of men in a panic. All forward movement in the Roman lines was abruptly forgotten. Even some of the fleeing Celts and Iberians rallied, driving back the attacking Romans, whose momentum came to a halt as they realised that something extraordinary was happening.

Monomachos and Qarthalo had led their Libyans into the Roman flanks. The trap had sprung at last.

For a moment, Hannibal sagged with relief so profound that it felt like vertigo.

They had won. Cornelius Lentulus was roaring out his wild triumph
along with the men around him, charging after retreating and fleeing
Celts and Iberians, trying to force his horse forward past the slower,
crowded infantrymen, hacking at enemy backs and shoulders whenever he
could reach them.

He was brought to an abrupt halt as something crashed into his horse. The
animal shied and jumped, to avoid stepping on a knot of *principes* that had

somehow been knocked directly in front of him. Confused, Lentulus looked to his right, where Roman soldiers were trying to pick themselves up from the ground, one of them stammering an excuse for the tribune (or so Lentulus surmised). One got back to his feet, and stumbled again, this time over a dead Iberian. For the most fleeting of moments, Lentulus wondered if this had been one of Hannibal's ploys – to hamper them, by having them clamber over dead bodies.

Don't say the name. It's unlucky.

Suddenly he saw, further to the right, that the entire mass of legionaries was in motion, reminding Lentulus of a roof full of tiles, all sliding as one of them was knocked off. He realised only now how incredibly tightly packed they

were. Men were crowding against him, nearly pinning his leg against his horse. Frightened, the animal tried to break out. There was a scream as it stepped on someone.

That first sensation of confusion turned into horror as he realised that something incomprehensible was going on, starting on the far right of the field. Even above the din of cries and ringing metal, another sound was suddenly heard, higher, far away but carried over by a relentless wind. Screams of fear. He couldn't see what caused them. He could only hear them, and as he looked around, he saw the same expression on every face in the crowded mass around him, caught in different stages between puzzlement and panic.

Everyone around him swayed again. He heard shouts from the other side, saw fleeing soldiers turning, their fear changing to confusion as the enemy, too, tried to realise what was happening. Already, a few centurions with a better overview – or just, by pure chance, with some freedom of movement remain-ing – tried to push forward, out of the swaying mass.

But then the enemy realised that something unexpected had happened, that the Roman line was in disarray, no longer presenting a solid front and pa-cked so close that some men could barely use their weapons. With a sense of mount-ing horror, Lentulus suddenly was under the impression that the enemy had even waited for this. Celts and Iberians raised war cries, scattered at first, then more of them, and then, pandemonium broke loose. Men in front of Lentulus fell to enemy swords and spears, almost helpless as the Carthaginians attacked again, too close to the next man to use their shields effectively. Those who were hit by enemy blades tried to shrink back into the safety of the line, adding to the pushing and reeling in the centre, presenting their unprotected sides. The space all around seemed to become even more crowded with every moment.

Lentulus cast around wildly for Paullus. He realised he must have charged ahead of the consul, and it took him a while to pick out the red cloak in all the chaos around him, some thirty feet behind. Paullus had slipped off his horse in the commotion. Centho was trying to help him mount again, but an Iberian in front of him thrust him back with his shield, lunging at the consul. Lentulus fought to get his mount under control. The animal's eyes were rolling in panic; realising he would never make it in time, Lentulus threw himself off his horse's back. He was flung to the side, and felt a snap in his left arm.

Dizzily, he lay on the ground, watching his horse stamp over him, barely missing his right hand. Other legionaries were moving around them in what seemed to Lentulus like a surpassingly bizarre dance. He couldn't pull away. His left arm was a blaze of pain. It was still strapped to his shield, the shield hemmed in somehow, but he couldn't move his arm, couldn't pull free. The dance continued. More pain exploded along his left arm as someone fell ac-ross him. He felt blackness welling up at the edge of his field of vision, and for one heartbeat, he wanted to succumb to it. He thought about his mother, about his father, and wondered if they would even know how he had died.

Maybe they would just hope for news, and stop waiting at some point.

Survival instinct kicked in then, even stronger than the pain, and Lentulus scrambled backwards, thrusting himself off with his feet and managing to push the writhing body off him. A stab of agony, and his arm was free. With his right, he managed to grab a hard object, the edge of a shield maybe, and pulled himself up. Up was the way to go. To fall was to be trampled.

His senses reeling, Lentulus tried to orient himself, but was pressed to the side; there were men crashing into him, and he was being pushed further away from Paullus. He briefly caught sight of the red cloak, saw it hit by a spear, shouted at the consul, then he reeled again, fighting to just remain standing. There were muffled screams from below him, and to his horror, he realised he was treading on something soft. He tried to get off whatever he was standing on, scrambling away in a sense of mounting panic, until he was pushed into something solid behind him. Shield, man, horse, he wasn't sure which. He blinked back sweat clogged with dust or blood or tears; he couldn't see the consul, or Centho, or Furius, or Servilius. Suddenly, what had only moments before been a well-ordered battle line, and then a victorious army in pursuit, had turned into mindless chaos.

The solid thing behind him turned out to be a horse. It wasn't his, he saw that much, but he didn't care.

On the left wing of the field, Terentius Varro was beginning to feel he was achieving nothing. His allied cavalry was still fighting valiantly, but what use was valour when faced with the fast hit-and-run actions of an enemy that never got close? He had had little trouble to cheer on his men, but had hardly exchanged a single blow. Instead, the showers of spears which the Numidians cast at every pass seemed endless, wearing away at their men and horses, and, slowly but surely, at their fighting spirits. Several times in the two or three hours that the fighting must have lasted, Varro had tried to push in, force the opponent to close quarters combat, but they were too fast, evading, always evading him, breaking up in small units, racing away, reforming again. He had even tried to disengage, to bring aid to the infantry as it became clear that the battle would not be over as soon as everyone had hoped – but the Numidians didn't let him, swooping over them like so many shepherd dogs herding a flock of sheep in whatever direction they pleased. Still, he told himself, he was achieving no mean thing – he might not lead his troops to rout the enemy, but at least he was neutralising part of Hannibal's legendary cavalry.

His delusions were shattered when a clamour went up behind them, and incredulously, Varro saw the first Campanians breaking in the rear ranks.

He turned his horse and raced back along the line, shouting at terrified rid-ers to stand and fight. His bodyguard could barely keep up with him. His appearance did have the effect to prevent more men from fleeing, but what Varro saw when he reached the last ranks was enough to make the staunchest man's heart stop.

Seemingly from nowhere, although reasoning told him they must have routed the citizen cavalry and then ridden around the Roman rear, the Punic heavy cavalry had come. The sheer mass of them had sent his own men fleeing even before the lines could clash. The fright of men and animals overrode duty and oaths of loyalty as most of the men under his *vexillum* turned tail.

The tribunes were bellowing orders, threatening to turn their swords upon the fleeing. One of them was simply run over; the others were easy to sweep past. Suddenly, there were spears from behind them, spears from in front of them, as the Numidians came in for another attack. This broke the last shreds of resistance. It was a rout.

Varro saw it all like a sleeper unable to wake up from a nightmare, unable to move, unable to act. This was not happening. It could not be happening.

The centre. He needed to take as many of his men as he could and make for the centre.

He rounded up as many of the tribunes as he could see, as well as the remnants of his guard – one had been killed, two swept away with the fleeing men – and together, they slipped through between Iberian and Celtic cavalry from the north and Numidian from the south, making for the main battle line.

There was no line.

What Varro saw, almost convincing him that this was indeed a terrible dream, were ranks of legionaries facing inwards, attacking their own comrades from the flanks. As he got closer, the true horror hit him.

They weren't legionaries at all, but Africans, some of them armoured in looted suits of mail and breastplates and Roman helmets and shields, and they had surrounded the Roman centre, relentlessly pushing inwards, cutting down all in their path.

The dented centre. They had been looking at the Carthaginian's ambush all along. By some sort of witchcraft, he had hidden it in plain view. In his damned dented centre.

Feeling helpless and faint, Varro turned his mount and looked around wildly. Behind, Carthaginian foot soldiers were crushing the lines. To his left, enemy heavy cavalry were cutting down the few that had stood to fight to the end. Ahead, the Numidians were sweeping up the ones who tried to run.

A group of Samnite horsemen was racing towards them, aimlessly, trying to escape hammer and anvil. A squadron of Numidians was pursuing them; Varro heard one of them cry something over and over, which he recognised as a Barbarian garbled version of *consul*.

The men around him prepared for a last stand. Even some of the Samnites joined their desperate ranks, whether they actually hoped to escape that way or whether they had chosen their favoured way to die, Varro didn't know. The Numidians drew up short as they were faced with solid resistance, and in that short break, Varro and his few followers rushed against them, sweeping them aside, ducking under a hail of thrown spears, and before he even knew whether this was something desirable, the path to the south was free.

None of them said a word as they raced away, even much later, when they knew they had long shaken off pursuit – as if, by not talking about it, they could make their flight any less real.

The Roman allied cavalry had broken, and everyone who still had a horse under him was fleeing. The Numidians were already giving chase. Hasdrubal cursed as he saw that his men were about to give in to the overwhelming urge to pursue. He grabbed the horn-blower.

"Sound the rally!"

The man stared at him, his face flushed, uncomprehending. Hasdrubal saw that he was on the verge of asking why, until he realised he had been given an order, and obeyed.

"Find Hanno!" Hasdrubal shouted at one of his aides, and the man raced off.

Hasdrubal was relieved to see that most of his men – though not all; a flush of victory must have got the better of a few of the Celts – were obeying the order, though with expressions ranging from bewilderment to contemplated mutiny.

"Hanno!" he bellowed, looking around for the general's nephew.

The man who turned his horse was not Hanno, but one of his Numidian junior officers, by the name of Gulussa. His eyes were wide in triumph mixed with irritation as he looked at Hasdrubal for an explanation.

"Where's Hanno?" Hasdrubal demanded.

"Wounded," Gulussa replied. "A spear. I don't know how bad. They're taking him to the camp."

Hasdrubal cursed. "Gulussa, I'm leaving you in charge of the pursuit. I've still got work to do. Got a string to pull on a bag of rats." He saw Gulussa's puzzled look, but there would be time for explanations later. And if anyone ever dared to call him "Hasdrubal the Ratter" in public, noses would bleed.

Not even waiting to see whether the Numidian obeyed his order, Hasdrubal turned his horse, and gathered his men together. He ordered them to form up in a long column, and then led them back the way they had come.

The Roman rear was in disorder. The rearmost ranks had been sucked in, breaking formation, when the front ranks had pushed against Hannibal's line and pressed inward. Normally, the last ranks should have been made up of *triarii*, the most seasoned of veterans, and when they presented a shield wall, a cavalry charge against those was a nightmare at best, impossible at worst. In fact, Hasdrubal had already decided that he would have his men dismount to attack on foot, or just close off escape routes without attacking at all.

Before he could give the order, however, he saw that barely every tenth man in the Roman ranks wore the mail coat of a *triarius*. Instead, he saw men wearing animal skins on their heads, the occasional spear, shields but no armour. The withdrawn *velites* were milling around in the confusion that was spreading through the Roman ranks as the flank attack of the Libyans became clear. As yet, they didn't know for sure what was going on, hadn't realised yet that they were not merely facing a defeat, but utter disaster.

Encountering almost no ordered opposition, Hasdrubal hit the rear line with a force that sent shockwaves into the very centre of the infantry. Encirclement was complete.

Servilius Geminus was dead, hacked to pieces by several Iberian swords at once. Furius Bibaculus was dying, run through with a spear. Claudius Centho was dead, defending the consul, who was bleeding from half a dozen wounds, blearily staring around himself in a state of shock and utter disbelief. The legates' bodyguards were simply cut down along with them. Lentulus had drifted into view and out again, shouting at him, but the words had made no sense.

Aemilius Paullus had left the dying right flank, only to die in the centre.

The Spanish and Celtic swordsmen, who by every sensible account had already lost the battle, had renewed their attacks with the senseless vigour of blood rage, and the legions, who mere moments before had thought them-

selves the sure winners, were reduced to a panicked, stumbling, bleeding mass that was cut down without any focused opposition. Escape was impossible. There were pockets of resistance, where the men still had enough space to simply remain standing and even defend themselves; but as the enemy pushed in again, it was soon seen that this was nothing but the last dying gasp of the formidable Roman army.

All around Paullus, men were being pushed against each other by forces that defied any comprehension, stumbling and falling, trampling their own comrades as they tried to get up. There were attempts to push in one direction to break free from the cramped quarters, in a more coordinated way,

where centurions still managed to make themselves heard; one would always stumble, dragging down others. Some would try to bend down to pull up fallen comrades, brothers or friends; to bend down was to lose footing and be dragged down with the ones they were trying to help.

It was a scene from a nightmare, something conjured up from the horrors of Tartarus, something that the mind could not comprehend. Sooner or later, the Carthaginians came to end it. At some point, the will to fight was simply quenched, and the will to live followed not long after. The men who had set

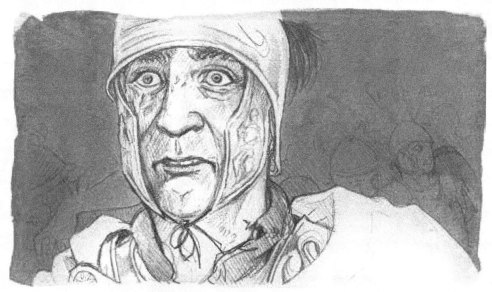

out to crush the army of Carthage were finding themselves helpless, powerless, utterly unable to fight back. Numbly, Paullus saw men lying with their chests crushed or broken limbs, half-buried under the dead and dying, begging to be killed by their own comrades, some complying, some too dazed. Despite his many wounds, Paullus felt no pain. His entire body was numb, nerveless. Wounds felt insignificant compared to what his eyes were seeing. He blinked, again and again, wanting to close his eyes to the dread around him. And yet, he couldn't. He had led these men onto this field of blood. It was his duty now to watch them die.

Something hit him, then something else. He didn't care what it had been. Images flashed across his consciousness, of Valeria, his wife, and his children, Aemilia and Lucius, playing with walnuts on the hot stone steps in front of the house, the blue summer sky above them as Valeria watched. The images were peaceful. He wanted to keep them with him, but they didn't belong here.

He didn't feel himself falling, only found himself lying on his back, and the last thing he saw was that blue, blue sky.

A group of Celts stalked past Bomilkar, past Hannibal and what remained of his guard, into the centre, which had become one gigantic butcher's yard.

Desperate perseverance had turned to triumph in what had seemed like the blink of an eye, and had released energies that hardly anyone would have believed were still there. There was barely any need for exhorting the soldiers anymore; the entire field had been swept up by an invisible, compelling drive. *Inward.*

Bomilkar had been a soldier for almost twenty years. On Hannibal's campaigns, and those of his father and brother-in-law before him, he had seen the carnage that followed the heady first moments of victory. He had seen thorough defeats of enemy forces. This, he was sure, was something that no living soul could ever have experienced. It was unthinkable that any force as large as this had ever been completely encircled, much less by one inferior in numbers, and been so completely crushed.

The butchery that followed victory was always ugly, always messy, always dreadful. This was unfathomable. And there seemed to be no end to it. There existed some point after a battle when the senseless focus that coated the self with a protective layer of battle rage and undiscerning bloodlust receded, and the self re-emerged, either drunk on victory or numb with exhaus-tion, often both. A moment when a veil suddenly seemed to have been drawn aside, and the sounds and smells and sights that had hitherto been blocked out all flooded in at once. Normally, when that moment came, the fighting simply ceased, little by little, until there was nobody left anyway that could be fought. Usually, in Bomilkar's experience, that happened within an hour of the onset of the slaughter, often considerably sooner if enemies fled or surrendered.

That point came, and went. The

hours came and went. Even the sun went, as if he had seen enough.

And still the inward movement forced them on.

So many. They lay in heaps, or fell in heaps, sometimes with no ground around them to walk on except the bodies. Where there was ground to walk on, it was no longer the pale yellow colour that it had been, but was slick with dark blood. Bomilkar's horse – the fourth or fifth he had ridden since this morning; he had stopped counting – just refused to go on at one point, refusing to step among the bodies and the carnage; mechanically, he dismounted and continued on foot.

Just a few hours ago, Bomilkar had heard Hannibal say that not a single Gisgo stood on the Roman side of the field. Now, he numbly wondered how many thousand Gaiuses, Marcuses, or Gnaeuses lay here.

So many. There seemed to be no end to it. Some very few still presented a fighting front. Some of them managed to retreat, shields facing the enemy, moving in a closed formation as the killers went for easier prey. Many had been trampled or crushed to death in the mass panic that had broken out in the centre after encirclement; many were still alive, some wounded, others too weak or too deep in shock to offer resistance. There was little surrender. Bomilkar saw a few raising their hands and shouting something; after the third or fourth time, he recognised it as *desine* or *desinite*. Once or twice, the meaning of the words and gestures registered only after he had pushed his sword into their necks. His feet and hands seemed to do the work of their own accord, without leaving him a say in the matter. Some he just went past if he judged them no threat, preserving his energy and the mercy of his sword for the ones who might be.

So many. Once or twice, he slipped in the slick mire that the dusty field had turned into. When he pushed himself up again, sometimes the bodies he was leaning on were still moving. In some places, he had to clamber. His feet were blackish red up over his ankles, and there were fat blue flies everywhere now, buzzing up in clouds when a body shifted, and settling on his blood-smeared hands and face before he mechanically brushed them away. It was useless. They were back immediately.

It was all tendons and shoulders and bellies, some men already lying dead by their own swords or those of their friends, some just offering their necks. One had burrowed his face into the earth to suffocate himself.

Bomilkar fell to his hands and knees and was violently sick.

He would never have made it without the horse.

Lentulus clung to the horse as he clung to consciousness, and didn't see much else. He was adrift in an ocean that was the stuff of nightmares, and that was all he wanted to know, needed to know. He didn't try to direct the animal; it did that on its own, picking its path instinctively amid the jostling and pushing. He didn't know how long. He had lost his sword, and his shield. Something inside him insisted that he should feel ashamed of this fact, but the rest of him didn't care. Once or twice, someone tried to talk to him, but he barely heard.

Suddenly, the crowd and screams lessened; he was carried away in a small trickle of others that had found something precious, something incredible: direction. Around him, others were staggering, some pushing, some stalking along blearily, but all with the same goal. He didn't know what goal that was, but it was incredible enough that it was possible to move, together, with a purpose.

Much later, when he pieced together the shambles of the day, he understood that the trickle of fugitives that had taken him out of the slaughter had led him through one of the last gaps in the encirclement, somewhere between the Celts and Iberians, before the ring had been closed completely and all escape had become impossible.

The horse carried him for maybe a mile and a half before he rolled off its back.

It was getting dark when he regained consciousness. The first thing he saw were men around him, about a dozen. They were dead, with wounds in their necks and their backs, killed on the run. The enemies must have mistaken him for dead in their midst, so nobody had wasted a spear on him. They'd taken his cuirass and helmet, and left him. The horse was gone.

One of the men was looking at Lentulus, and he realised that this one was still alive. His legs had been hewn from under him. He said nothing, his eyes wide.

Shaking, Lentulus crawled near, tugged a spear out of a dead man's back and thrust it into the neck of the one before him.

He told himself that he saw a fleeting expression of gratitude cross the dying soldier's face.

Lentulus remained crouching there for a moment, contemplating the spear. Then he set it on the ground, leaning on it as he tried to get up. With his broken arm, he couldn't crawl, so he would have to walk.

It was easier than he had thought, rid of his armour. He stumbled a few times, but managed to fall on his right arm every time, and got up again leaning on the spear.

Water splashed against his feet, and he realised how thirsty he was. He dropped to his knees and brought up handful after handful of water, gobbling it down greedily.

It had a metallic taste to it.

Horror struck him as he saw, in the fading sunset, that the water ran red. Retching, he heaved it all up again until there could not be anything left in him, then he curled up in a ball, drenched and suddenly shivering with cold. He wished he still had his *paludamentum*, but the enemies had taken the cloak, too.

He tottered to his feet again, stumbling several times before he had reached the more even ground, away from the river. He staggered on, following the river downstream.

He had gone this way for an hour when he heard voices. Before he could think about what he was doing, he scrambled back down the riverbank, dropping into the rushes, his heart pounding, clutching the spear.

Fear gripped him when he realised that the voices were not speaking Latin, but then he recognised their language. Oscan. Fearing he had misheard, he remained lying for a while longer until he saw them. There were six of them, four Samnite horsemen, now without their horses, and two legionaries, *triarii* by their armour, half running, half stumbling, downriver, just like him.

Lentulus wanted to get up, but his legs wouldn't obey him.

Afraid they would run on and leave him alone, he croaked, as loudly as he could, "Help me!"

The looks in their eyes were wild, suspicious, as they turned to the river-

bank. Two of the Samnites and one of the Romans did not approach him, still fear-ing traps. The other three dragged him from the water. He sobbed as one of them jarred his left arm, and lay shivering on the riverbank.

"Who are you?" the *triarius* who had fished him out asked him, helping him to sit. His accent said rural Latium, not Rome.

"Gnaeus Cornelius Lentulus," Lentulus whispered. "Of the Fifth Legion."

"The Fifth?" the other exclaimed. He came closer now. "Lentulus the tribune?"

Lentulus nodded.

"Any news of Aemilius Paullus?" the *triarius* urged. "Did he escape? Do you know?"

Lentulus felt sick as he remembered, of all the horrors he had seen, a spear slamming into a red cloak. He tried to speak, but no words came. He suddenly thought of his mother and father again, and the look of joy he saw on their faces in his mind's eye turned to one of contempt and disgust when they learned that he had fled. His throat constricted as he realised he would never be able to explain to them what the field of Cannae had been like. There was no way he could ever make anyone understand who hadn't been here.

One of the Samnites thrust a leather flask into his hand. The liquid inside was *posca*, the watered-down sour wine that they all drank and detested, consul to slave. It was the temperature of piss, but Lentulus had never tasted anything so good.

"The consul?" the other *triarius* asked again when he had drunk. "Does he live?"

Lentulus shook his head.

He saw their faces. They were all here without their arms, without their shields. They all had forsaken their standards. They had all broken their oaths. And yet, he was a tribune. He could see that they expected him, if not themselves, to have had a good reason for turning tail and running.

Cornelius Lentulus was not a coward. He had not betrayed Aemilius Paullus.

He clung to the thought that there was nothing else he could have done for the consul.

The words just came tumbling out of him, without any pause to think. "I found him sitting on a stone," he whispered. "He was bleeding. Wounded. I offered him my horse. I wanted to guide him to safety. I told him to save his own life, to return to Rome, and not to despair of the Republic. He forbade it. He told me to save myself. Told me to ride to Rome and tell the senate – tell the senate that Lucius Aemilius Paullus stayed true to the Republic until the end."

They didn't ask any further.

Gnaeus Cornelius Lentulus stuck to this story until the day he died.

It sounded like something Aemilius Paullus would have said if he had had the chance.

The sun went down in a blood-red haze, and darkness finally settled over the plain of Cannae.

The sweltering heat of the day had passed, and it was growing quiet again. The quiet was different from ordinary summer evenings. There were no crickets. They seemed to be scared away by the stench of blood. The only sounds came from the battlefield every now and then, of those who had been forgotten, and the occasional *caw* of crows, squabbling over the best morsels.

The slaughter had finally ceased, but Hannibal was still on the field. His body felt like lead, his head seemed to have no weight at all. Part of it was the familiar but still peculiar sensation of removing a helmet after a day of wearing it without pause; part of it was a curious combination of fatigue and elation and blood loss and horror and relief, which seemed to completely neutralise each other and leave nothing behind in their place.

Mago was suddenly beside him, pulling him into an embrace which almost sent him staggering. When he let him go, Hannibal saw the same dazed expression on his brother's face, like a man sleepwalking who expected to wake up from a bizarre dream any moment. Maharbal was with him, inexplicably soaked head to toe, shaking his head and laughing and cursing and again shaking his head as he, too, embraced him. Mago's face looked a mess; there was a bleeding gash across his cheek, but he didn't seem to notice. His hand jerked up as if to embrace Hannibal once more, then he let it sink again as if he was afraid to touch him. "We –" he began, broke off, then started again, "This – *you* –"

"Yes." Hannibal felt he ought to say more, but his voice was so hoarse that he couldn't have, even if he could have thought of anything. "Yes." He pulled Mago close again, briefly resting his face against his brother's, and found the younger was shaking. Or maybe it was both of them. He barely could tell. He could hardly believe that they had made it through alive.

They had won. Hannibal had to repeat it to himself, again and again. They had won. The Roman army was no more. They had done the impossible, had completely encircled and all but annihilated four consular armies in a single battle, outnumbered three to five. No matter how often he repeated it, the thought just bounced off his brain, refusing to sink in.

"By all the gods," said Maharbal, "I wish you could have seen it, Hannibal – really seen it, from up there – it had something... geometrical to it."

"I *have* seen it."

"It's over," Maharbal went on, a fire burning in his eyes. "They'll have to seek terms now. There's no way they can keep up the war. We'll send – "

"Yes," Hannibal said again, slightly sharper in tone, cutting him short. It was the fourth step before the second. Maharbal hadn't been here, in the middle of the madness; for him, it had been a faraway, rational thing, coloured wooden blocks on a map. He couldn't fault him for rational thinking, and racing through conclusions. But it was too soon for that. Much too soon. There were thousands of half-dead men lying here, Romans and his own.

Maharbal took the hint. Hannibal listened to his more sober reports of the cavalry battle, Hasdrubal's initiative, the repelled attack on the camp, Hanno's injury, Gulussa's pursuit of the fleeing cavalry, the flight of Terentius Varro, reports of high-ranking Roman dead, among them Aemilius Paullus. As soon as Maharbal was finished, Hannibal got to work, caught in a restless, feverish blur of activity.

He sent junior officers to gather together their men and find their wounded for a first tentative overview of losses. He ordered groups of Numidian, Iberian and Celtic horsemen, who were the least exhausted, to help the medics to get the severely wounded off the battlefield, and the more lightly wounded to the camp. He went to see Hanno and found him in the care of the physicians. They said the spear wound to his shoulder would mend, given time. In the camp, men were celebrating, raising cheers and chants as they saw him. But

even the ones who were cheering seemed dazed by what they had just taken part in.

Back on the field, Hannibal dispatched a Libyan contingent, together with a few Celtic chieftains who knew the consul from sight, to search for the bodies of Aemilius Paullus and the other high-ranking Roman officers, to be given honourable burials. From prisoners, he had learned that Servilius Geminus and Minucius Rufus, both quaestors, and what must be dozens of senators were among the dead. He sent another contingent of riders for fresh water from upriver. He ordered Maharbal to find out how many of the Roman garrisons – and fugitives from the battle – had taken refuge in the camps, and how to deal with them. He conversed with Hasdrubal about tentative ideas of how to dispose of the staggering number of dead. He did not even have

estimates at this stage, but it was apparent they would number in the tens of thousands on the Roman side alone, possibly as many as sixty thousand. It was a number that defied logic. Even if he put every one of his own men that was unhurt to the task, it would take a week to dig pits and cremate all the bodies, by which time they would long have begun to rot in the Apulian sun. Neither he nor Hasdrubal could come up with any solution.

In between, his physician found him, cleaned his wounds with sour wine, and cauterised the one in his thigh. Hannibal didn't even sit down for it, leaning on Mago during the procedure, and afterwards, he immediately got back to work, afraid of sitting down, knowing that once he did, it would become impossible to get up again. Some time after sunset, Mago brought him water and something to eat. He wolfed it down without registering what it was.

The sun had long set when he finally sent the last of the men back to the camp, to celebrate, or to rest. There had been some looting, but unusually little yet. The exhausted victors had left the field in the macabre certainty that everything would still be there on the morrow. The crows had taken over, swarms of them, despite the late hour, partaking in a feast that was too good to be missed. As opposed to the soldiers, they could not understand that this feast would last them for days.

The men, too, would be back tomorrow, for the most terrible task – to kill the severely wounded who survived the night on the battlefield.

Slowly and still somewhat inadvertently, as if his feet had decided to finally take the matter upon themselves, he began to walk back to the riverbank, and came to a halt by the water's edge.

The camp on the other side, with its burning fires and still ongoing celebra-

tions, beckoned irresistibly. Rest seemed like celebration in itself. But he was unable to leave this place. Just standing here, at the edge of the battlefield, by the murmuring river that swallowed the other sounds of the night, felt like an act of worship, an obligation to gods and men.

The soldiers had been working by torchlight; now, they were gone, and the torches with them. The sky was full of summer stars. Melqart was in their midst, so vast that he seemed to span half the sky.

Hannibal knelt, ignoring the sharp stab of pain in his thigh and waiting for the moment of light-headedness to pass; then he plunged his hands into the cool water, slowly and deliberately washing his feet, then his hands, and lastly scooping water over his face and head.

He brought up a handful of crumbling earth. It was colourless in the darkness, but his fingers sensed that it was red.

Tanit, face of Baal, mother of Qart-hadasht. Baal-Hammon, Lord of the incense altars. Melqart, king of the City and protector of my family. To you I offer up this victory won on the battlefield. You I ask to guide me in the days to come. Your help I pray to bring this war to a conclusion now. You I ask to bestow your grace on Qart-hadasht, and restore her honour and greatness.

As he released the handful of earth again, he felt more than saw Bomilkar standing a small distance away, watching him.

For a moment, Hannibal wearily prepared to ward off the chief guard's nagging to get him back to the camp. But Bomilkar just stood there, and said nothing.

He, too, must have felt the obligation to gods and men.

On the battlefield of Cannae, on 2nd
August 216 BC,
approximately 50,000 Romans were
killed.
Up to 20,000 were taken captive, less than
that number escaped.
Most of the latter were taken or fled
from the camps,
rather than from the battlefield itself.

Hannibal lost around 6,000 men, two-
thirds of them Celts.

Some time after the battle,
Hannibal sent an envoy to Rome,
to offer the ransoming of prisoners,
and offer peace terms.
He thought that Cannae would end the war.

The senate in Rome didn't even let his
embassy enter the city.

After Cannae, Rome's generals never dared
to meet Hannibal in open battle again,
until Publius Cornelius Scipio,
after successfully driving the
Carthaginians out of Iberia
in a series of tactically brilliant battles,
defeated Hannibal on the plain of Zama
in 202 BC.

Carthage stood for less than fifty more
years,
before it was burnt to the ground
by Publius Cornelius Scipio Aemilianus,
grandson of Lucius Aemilius Paullus.

APPENDICES

CHARACTERS

(an <u>underlined</u> name denotes that the character is historical)

CARTHAGINIANS AND ALLIES

Abartiaigis, one of Hannibal's guards (Iberian)

Alco, a junior officer (Iberian)

<u>**Barmokar**</u>, a councillor from Carthage

Bodeshmun, a junior officer

Bomilkar, chief guard

Bostar, one of Hannibal's guards

Gabrannos, a Gallic chieftain

<u>**Gisgo**</u>, Carthaginian infantry commander

Gulussa, a Numidian junior officer

<u>**Hamilkar Barca**</u> (†), father of Hannibal, Hasdrubal, and Mago Barca

<u>**Hannibal Barca**</u>, Carthaginian general

<u>**Hanno Barca**</u>, Hannibal's nephew

<u>**Hasdrubal Barca**</u>, Hannibal's brother, commanding the armies in Iberia

<u>**Hasdrubal the Fair**</u> (†), brother-in-law of Hannibal, general in Iberia after the death of Hamilkar Barca

<u>**Hasdrubal (the Ugly)**</u>, officer of the service corps and sometime cavalry commander

Himilko, one of Hannibal's guards

Ikorbas, a Balearic slinger

Italces, a dispatch rider

Iuba, a dispatch rider

<u>**Mago Barca**</u>, Hannibal's youngest brother

<u>**Mago**</u>, a councillor from Carthage

<u>**Maharbal**</u>, Hannibal's second in command and cavalry officer

Medesh, a dispatch rider

<u>**Monomachos**</u>, Carthaginian infantry commander

Mutumbal, a junior officer

<u>**Myrkan**</u>, a councillor from Carthage

<u>**Qarthalo**</u>, Carthaginian infantry commander

Sedaca, a junior officer (Iberian)

ROMANS

(names used in the narrative are in **bold**)

Marcus Claudius **Centho**, a military tribune

Lucius Aurelius **Cotta**, a military tribune

Quintus **Fabius** Maximus, Roman dictator; called Cunctator (Delayer), took over command following the disastrous defeat at Lake Trasimene in 217 BC (a year before Cannae)

Gaius **Flaminius** (†), consul of the previous year, died in the Battle of Lake Trasimene

Lucius **Furius** Bibaculus, a quaestor serving as Paullus' aide

Gnaeus Cornelius **Lentulus**, a military tribune

Gnaeus **Octavius**, a military tribune

Lucius Aemilius **Paullus**, Roman consul 216 BC

Lucius Calpurnius **Piso**, a military tribune

Appius Claudius **Pulcher**, a military tribune

Marcus Minucius **Rufus**, Roman legate in charge of the sixth and eighth legions

Publius Cornelius **Scipio**, a military tribune

Tiberius **Sempronius** Longus, consul of 218, lost the Battle of the Trebia against Hannibal

Gnaeus **Servilius** Geminus, Roman consul of 217 BC; legate at Cannae, in charge of the fifth and seventh legions

Gaius Terentius **Varro**, Roman consul 216

GLOSSARY

Africa – the Roman name for the coastal strip between modern Morocco and Tunisia, called "Libya" in Greek

Apulia – a region in southern Italy, on the Adriatic coast

augur – a Roman official in charge of interpreting birds' behaviour as omens

auspices – foretelling the future by birds' behaviour

Baal – a name of several gods of Carthage (meaning "Lord"), mainly the chief gods Baal Hammon and Baal Shamim

Baleareans – inhabitants of the Baleares, serving as slingers in the Punic army

Barcid – pertaining to Hamilkar Barca and his family

Bellona – female Roman deity of war

Campania – a region in southern Italy

Carthage – a great city in North Africa. Punic name: Qart-hadasht

Castor and Pollux – Roman (demi) gods

centurion – a Roman officer of a century

century – Roman unit of 60 men

consul – the highest office in the Roman Republic, held by two men elected for one year

cornicen *(pl. cornicines)* – a Roman horn-blower

decurion – leader of thirty Roman riders

dictator – a magistrate elected for six months in a time of crisis

Etruria – a region in central Italy

falcata – curved Iberian sword

Gaetulans – a people indigenous to North Africa

haruspex *(pl. haruspices)* – a Roman official foretelling the future from the liver of a sacrificial animal

hastatus (pl. hastati) – the soldiers in the first proper battle-line of a Roman infantry centre; some of the youngest soldiers

Iberia – ancient name for Spain

Illyria – the region along the Adriatic opposite Italy, where Aemilius Paullus fought a local ruler in 219 BC

Insubri – a Celtic tribe inhabiting the Po valley, allied with Hannibal

lararium – a small shrine usually found in a Roman house but sometimes taken on campaign by higher-ranking officials, at which the "personal gods" were worshipped

lares – the deified spirits of the departed; the ancestors

Latium – the area around Rome

legate – commander of a legion, usually of consular or proconsular rank

legion – a contingent of usually 4,200 soldiers, complemented by a similar number of auxiliary troops, thus bringing it to about 9,000 men. At Cannae, the legions had been brought up to 4,600 men each, resulting in the overall number of ca. 86,000 Roman soldiers on the field

Libya – The coastal strip around Carthage, called "Africa" by the Romans

Libyphoenicians – people from North Africa, result of intermingling between Phoenicians and native Libyans

Lucania – a region in southern Italy

maniple – a unit of 120 Roman legionaries (two centuries)

Melqart – a Phoenician god associated with Herakles

Moors – a people indigenous to North

Africa

Numidians – a people settling in North Africa, mainly in today's Algeria, famed for their superior horsemen

Oretani – a Spanish tribe settling in South Iberia; erstwhile enemies of Carthage

Oscan – a language spoken in southern Italy

paludamentum – a Roman officer's cloak

pilum *(pl. pila)* – Roman throwing spear

pontifex – a priest in Roman state religion (as opposed to other societies, secular and spiritual power in Rome were often combined in the same person)

princeps *(pl. principes)* – heavily armed foot soldiers, making up the second battle line in the Roman infantry

proconsul – the previous year's consul

Punic (usually as adjective) – Carthaginian

quaestor – a Roman magistrate, here serving as aide to a consul

Qart-hadasht – the name of Carthage in Punic

Samnites – a tribe in southern Italy, allied with Rome

Searo – a small town in southern Iberia

Shadrapha – a Punic god of health

signifer – Roman standard-bearer

stade – Greek unit of length, measuring around 170 metres

Tagus – a river in Iberia, where Hannibal won his first victory as general in 220 BC

Tanit – patron goddess of Carthage, also named "Face of Baal"

Thermopylai – site of a battle in 480 BC, in which a small Spartan army defeated a huge Persian host

Trasimene – a lake in Etruria where Hannibal defeated the Roman army under consul Gaius Flaminius in 217 BC by hiding his entire army in an ambush along the lake-shore

Trebia – a river in the Po valley where Hannibal beat the Romans under Sempronius Longus in 218 BC

triarius *(pl. triarii)* – the oldest and most experienced Roman soldiers, forming the last battle line

turma *(pl. turmae)* – a unit of thirty Roman riders

tribune, military – a junior officer of noble birth in the Roman army (each legion had six)

veles *(pl. velites)* – the youngest and most inexperienced Roman soldiers, fighting as lightly-armed skirmishers in a long line before the centre proper

vexillum – (1) the standard of a Roman consul, put up in front of his tent as a sign for battle; (2) the standard of a Roman cavalry unit

via principalis – one of the main roads crossing a Roman camp

264-241 First war between Rome and Carthage.

late 247 Hannibal born as the eldest son of Hamilkar Barca.

237 Rome occupies the formerly Carthaginian possessions of Sardinia and Corsica. Hamilkar leads an army to Iberia; Hannibal (9) comes with him.

229 Hamilkar dies in Iberia; succeeded by his son-in-law, Hasdrubal the Fair.

221 Hannibal succeeds Hasdrubal as general of Iberia and Africa.

218 War between Rome and Carthage breaks out over a disputed town in Iberia. Hannibal marches from Iberia through Gaul and across the Alps into Italy. He beats both Roman consuls within two months.

217 Hannibal beats the army of consul Gaius Flaminius at Lake Trasimene. Quintus Fabius Maximus then declines to fight Hannibal at all.

216 Hannibal completely destroys four consular armies at Cannae.

215-204 In Italy, Hannibal conquers several towns after Rome reverts to the Fabian strategy of avoiding battle; Rome retakes them as soon as his back is turned. In Iberia, the war slowly turns to favour Rome, and Publius Cornelius Scipio. In 204, Iberia is lost, and Hannibal is recalled to Carthage when Scipio threatens it directly.

202 At Zama, Scipio defeats Hannibal and receives the honorary name "Africanus".

201 Peace treaty.

196 Hannibal achieves a number of political and financial reforms in Carthage, which antagonize members of the aristocracy.

195-183 Denounced by political opponents, Hannibal is forced to flee Carthage, and finds refuge with a series of Hellenistic kings, always pursued by Rome. He finally ends his own life with poison.

149-146 Rome instigates the Third Punic War, which ends with the utter destruction of the city.

Acknowledgements

I would like to offer thanks to the many people whose help contributed to this book:

Helmut Schulz, the greatest beta reader, idea-bouncer, tactical and artistic critic that any creative person could wish for.

Erin Clark and Scott Washburn for extremely helpful and constructive criticism.

Ricarda Truchseß, for putting up with my naïve ideas about layout, and pulling it off despite my interference.

Petra Nepomuck, whose enthusiasm and hands-on help was utterly refreshing.

Ben Kane, for his support and interest in the project, and the continued flow of inspiration from his reenactment photos.

Yozan Mosig, for sparking many, many interesting discussions. Yozan, I've borrowed a battering ram from you. I promise to return it in good condition.

The people at Geschichtsforum.de, who followed this project before it even was a project, and whose support and incredibly erudite advice meant a lot.

The people at Comicforum.de, who were extremely helpful with publication and layout ideas. And no, sorry, still no women!

The people at historum.com and romanarmytalk.com, and quite a few on Facebook, who have been very helpful with archaeological and technical details in arms and armour.

HISTORICAL NOTE

Nearly all of the main characters and events in this work are historical, or have been created in a way to fit in with the ancient descriptions of the battle of Cannae, and the Second Punic War.